Creatively CRUSHED

RECKLESS BASTARDS MC — MAYHEM, NV

WALL STREET JOURNAL & USA TODAY BESTSELLING AUTHOR

KB WINTERS

Copyright and Disclaimer

This book is a work of fiction. The names, characters, places and incidents are products of the writer's imagination and have been used fictitiously and are not to be construed as real. Any resemblance to persons, living or dead, actual events, locales or organizations is entirely coincidental.

Copyright © 2018 Book Boyfriends Publishing

All rights reserved. No part of this publication may be reproduced, stored in or introduced into a retrieval system, or transmitted, in any form, or by any means (electronic, mechanical, photocopying, recording, or otherwise) without the prior written permission of the copyright owner. The author acknowledges the trademarked status and trademark owners of various products referenced in this work of fiction, which have been used without permission. The publication/use of the trademarks is not authorized, associated with, or sponsored by the trademark owners.

Table of Contents

Copyright and Disclaimer ii

Chapter One 7

Chapter Two 15

Chapter Three 29

Chapter Four 37

Chapter Five 45

Chapter Six 57

Chapter Seven 79

Chapter Eight 97

Chapter Nine 111

Chapter Ten....................................... 125

Chapter Eleven.................................. 137

Chapter Twelve 145

Chapter Thirteen................................159

Chapter Fourteen 179

Chapter Fifteen 203

Chapter Sixteen................................. 209

Chapter Seventeen 233

Chapter Eighteen 253

Chapter Nineteen 263

Chapter Twenty 287

Chapter Twenty-One 305

Chapter Twenty-Two 315

chapter Twenty-Three 331

Chapter Twenty-Four 349

Chapter Twenty-Five 359

Chapter Twenty-Six 365

Chapter Twenty-Seven 375

Chapter Twenty-Eight 385

Chapter Twenty-Nine 405

Creatively Crushed

Reckless Bastards MC

By Wall Street Journal & USA Today Bestselling Author

KB Winters

CREATIVELY CRUSHED

Chapter One

Cross

"Where are all the bitches? I need my ego stroked," Stitch announced as he strolled up pulling a big ass cooler behind him.

I'd set everything up in the back where we had a grill and plenty of picnic tables, the perfect place for a cookout. Which was what I had planned for the Reckless Bastards tonight. "No Bitches, just the Bastards," I told him, greeting him with our handshake.

Stitch grinned wide like the easygoing guy he was. "Cool. I'll just have a shot of Patron and a beer to get started. You cooked?"

That was so typical of Stitch. The man was so relaxed all the time. He found happiness in the simple things, where I could barely remember what the simple things were.

Shit had been messy and complicated for so long that simple was a distant memory. Things got less and less simple as time went by, they got violent and bloody, dangerous and life-threatening. Not simple. Anything but simple, that was for fucking sure.

"No," I said, "the Bitches cooked and set everything up for us." Because it was their duty and they were happy to do it, but also because I bought them a night out at their favorite biker bar.

"Damn, lookin' good, Prez! With this spread I'm okay goin' without some lovin' from the ladies." Another laugh erupted from Stitch and he shot a playful frown at Golden Boy and Max as they arrived. "Old married dudes gotta wait, 'cause you fuckers get fed at home."

Max grinned and stole Stitch's beer when he was close enough. "My woman cooks all the time but she's painting with Moon and Rocky so this meal here is what I would call fortuitous."

CREATIVELY CRUSHED

"Yeah? Well I just came from Bungalow Three." Stitch's casually spoken words had the desired effect.

"Asshole." Max grunted out the word and shoved the bottle back into Stitch's hands before it ever touched his lips. "Glad I didn't have to kill you," he told the still laughing prospect who had more than proven himself over the past few years and took beers from the cooler, handing one to Golden Boy.

"My woman never cooks," Golden Boy offered after taking a long pull from the cold beer. "But she's oh so grateful when I do." Truth was that Golden Boy was a damn good cook and being with Teddy had helped him get his anger—at the club and the world— under control so it was nice to see the man he was before he'd spent six years in prison for a murder he didn't commit.

Max laughed along with his brother's innuendo, shaking his head. "So what you're saying is that you have to bribe your woman to fuck you?" It was good to see Max wearing a smile so easily. Before Jana came along I was pretty sure we'd lose him to his demons, his

PTSD that was pulling him further and further from the club and from life in general. But one petite blonde had changed all that.

My men, my brothers, were changing. They were improving, living better, happier lives. Except the club. The Reckless Bastards had seen a lot of shit over the past few years. Shit that made me question my own leadership skills, made me wonder if they would do better without me. I knew it was sad bastard talk but shit, some days I wanted to give up and run the fuck away.

Until I remembered that this club was the only fucking thing I had left in my life to care about. Without it, who knew what would happen to me. But I had a feeling that it wouldn't be pretty.

"Yo, Cross, what's up?" Gunnar strolled in just a few feet behind Jag, who hadn't been the same since his woman had been carted off by the CIA. All because she wanted to keep Jag and his brothers safe. Another instance where I failed my club. Gunnar wore his usual scowl.

CREATIVELY CRUSHED

"What's up is that we have food and booze for an unofficial meeting, so sit down, get comfortable and chill the fuck out." A wide smile spread across my face that I didn't feel, but it was intended to help everyone relax.

Except Jag, who grabbed a beer and set it in front of him, unopened, and stared off into the distance. There was nothing I could say to reach him, not now anyway. I didn't know if Jag blamed me but I knew that I did. Right now wasn't the time to get into it, but I would.

Soon.

"Things have been pretty fucked up around here lately," I began, hesitant at first.

"You can say that again!" Lasso whooped, wearing a big ass grin the size of Texas as he strode up to me and handed me a shot. "To our Prez, for getting every one of our sorry asses out alive. Every. Fucking. Time." His own shot glass was high in the air and the others joined in.

"Prez! Prez!" Gunnar pounded the table and the others joined in until they chanted so loud I could almost forget why we were gathered here tonight. Almost. Their praise only made me feel worse. Like a goddamn fraud.

I threw the shot back because I needed it and ten more, but for now the one would have to do. "We have more shit to walk through and then this city, Mayhem, will be ours." They cheered again, more amped up from the free booze and food than my words.

"These Roadkill assholes think they can come after us, after our women and our businesses and we won't fight back. They're wrong and I'm ready to prove to them just how wrong they were. It's gonna get ugly."

"No uglier than Jag's mug," Gunnar laughed and shoved Jag's shoulder, but the man didn't move. He didn't react.

"Really ugly and bloody as fuck. Then everyone will know that the Reckless Bastards are not to be fucked with!"

CREATIVELY CRUSHED

"Fuck yeah!" Lasso was energetic enough for the rest of us. It was definitely his wife Rocky who had taken the cocky playboy and turned him into a cocky ass family man who lived and breathed for his wife and son.

Everyone was happy. Everyone but me and Jag, though I had a feeling his unhappiness was a temporary thing whereas mine seemed to be a lifelong condition. Nevertheless, we sat around the tables, eating enough food to feed a small army, laughing and shooting the shit, making crude jokes the way men did when they were alone together. It was a good time.

A damn good time.

And if I had known what was coming, I would have savored that night even more.

KB WINTERS

Chapter Two

Moon

I loved Friday nights at my art shop. Mostly women showed up who wanted a different kind of night out. Tonight my own circle of friends gathered along with a bachelorette party and some regulars. The Rainbow Canvas sold art supplies as well as finished art in almost every medium imaginable. Local and even regional artists brought their creations to my little shop and gallery because they knew what I knew: art was subjective. Art that made one observer cry might make another wince, or recoil in disgust.

When everyone had gathered around me I said, "Okay ladies, tonight we have something a little different. Since you were a little too rambunctious for Mario last week, we have…well, let me just show you." I pulled back the sheet to show off the sketch I'd worked on all week.

"You have outdone yourself tonight, Moon." Jana smiled at the scene laid out for them. I did the outlines and the women filled it in.

"Thank you, Jana. Choose any portion you'd like to paint or take a crack at the entire thing. Ladies' choice tonight."

I went to the front room to turn on some low music—Creedence Clearwater Revival—and lock the door. The shop wasn't technically open this late and all the events were by reservation only. It was nice to be in a room filled with people having fun, doing normal things. I didn't have a lot of that in my life, not as the single parent of a child with severe asthma. But these nights, I did.

Rocky waved me over. "Hey Moon, come on over and chat with us!" A big sparkling grin on her face, red hair tumbling half way down her back because she hadn't cut it in months. Who had time with a four-month-old child at home?

"Hey Jana, Rocky. How's it going?"

CREATIVELY CRUSHED

"Good," Rocky began. "Now that I'm back to work, business has been better than ever, and Lasso promised to build a shed to keep my inventory in, *and* to keep baby Dallas out of said inventory." Her laugh was beautiful and melodic, bouncing off the walls and mingling with the beginning strains of *Bad Moon Rising*.

"How is little Dallas?" I hadn't seen him since he left the hospital, but I remember red curls covering pale, milky white skin and big blue eyes exactly like his cowboy daddy.

"Not so little. I swear he'll be bigger than me by the time he's six years old." She laughed affectionately, happiness written all over her face.

"And Jana, how is pregnancy number two treating you?" She smiled and some days I envied her, having a partner to help her through her pregnancies.

Her skin glowed beautifully. "I'll be happier than I can tell you when this one is out of me. Max has been overprotective as hell. Some days I'd like to kill him if it wouldn't leave me on my own with two children." She gave us a small chuckle that actually spoke volumes about her love for her guy.

"You know Lasso and I would help," Rocky offered up with a cheeky grin.

"Yeah thanks, Rocky." Jana rolled her eyes but I saw the barest hint of a smile she tried to hide. "What about you, Moon, are you seeing someone?"

"Not at all. Between the shop and Beau, my life is booked solid every single day." That was the truth, if not the whole truth. "Of the ones I have found, none of them have been worth rearranging my schedule for."

"Bullshit," Rocky said in her usually sharp way. "There's always time for love. Hell, I managed to find it while running for my life from a psycho, so I know of what I speak. You should listen to me."

"The difference, my crazy little friend, is that you came here for that man. Your paths were aligned to cross, which puts everything in an entirely different light."

CREATIVELY CRUSHED

"I'm calling bullshit again, but this time I'll say it with homemade peach soda. I made enough for three, Moon, even though you can still drink the hard stuff."

I didn't bother telling her I didn't drink often, mostly because people reacted strange to that bit of information. "I don't usually drink soda, so this is fantastic. Thank you, Rocky."

"Wait, hold the phone," Rocky said in her usually flamboyant way. "You don't drink soda? Like, at all?"

I shook my head with a smile. My aversion to sugar was another one that drew strange looks. "No. In fact—"

"How did I not know this? It makes a weird kind of sense, though so never mind. I'm no longer surprised."

Jana rolled her eyes before returning her gaze to the table in the center of the room. "Well I'd like to hear Moon's answer."

"Sugar increases inflammation, which can make Beau's asthma worse. I've never really been a fan and not having it in the house makes it easier all around. I don't want to run the risk of him getting into it by accident."

Jana's green eyes widened and then filled with apology. "Does that mean I shouldn't have brought the extra white chocolate lemon cake balls I made?"

My smile grew wide at her words. Both her concern and the gesture reminded me of what it was like before I avoided all connections with the world away from my son and my shop. Having girlfriends who gave out hugs for no particular reason, drinking and eating cake because being together was enough of a celebration. Those days were distant in my mind and hanging out with these women helped me remember.

"You definitely should have brought it. Lemon cake is my absolute favorite and your deserts have made me up my exercise game considerably."

Rocky laughed and squeezed my bare arms. "You do have pretty amazing guns. What do you do?"

CREATIVELY CRUSHED

"Yoga, Pilates, running. If Beau is up to it, we go bicycling." Despite his asthma, I wanted my son to have an appreciation for the outdoors. So far, it was a love affair.

"Does that mean I'm slacking?" Jana asked. "Because we go to the park. The end."

I lifted my bottle of peach soda in the air. "To good friends and doing the best you can."

"And to good soda," Rocky added with a wide smile and a wink.

"And to good times," Jana added, her giggle lighting up her whole face, which was on full display thanks to one of Rocky's homemade headbands she'd bought at a recent crafts night.

"To all that. And to art," I said seriously. "And the crazy creative fools who love it."

"Cheers!" Jana and Rocky shouted loudly, slamming the sturdy bottles together with a loud clang.

"Cheers again!" Several of the women from the bachelor party held up their own plastic wine glasses, narrowly missing expensive shoes and barely touched canvasses.

All the women were laughing and smiling, having a good time after putting in their forty hours or more at an office. It was a good feeling. Camaraderie. Belonging.

The sound of gunfire and breaking glass tore through the air and the room fell into caos. "Gun! Everyone down!"

My gaze darted around the room, searching the front of the shop where the larger windows allowed for a perfect view inside. A bright yellow car that looked a lot like Beau's favorite Transformer idled right in front of the broken glass and I stared at it for a long, terrifying moment.

More bullets flew, and I held my breath against the hard wood floor of the shop, easels and stools overturned. Several bottles of wine spilled over the table, staining the tablecloth, chairs and the floor below. An automatic sent a torrent of bullets raining down on us. It felt like they would never stop. The sounds of women screaming was all around me. I took several deep breaths, willing my body to remain calm. "Stay down!"

There it was. A brief reprieve. Silence, along with the distant metal-on-metal sound of a gun being reloaded, a sound I'd grown familiar with during my time in Panama. Then I heard it, another sound.

Gurgling.

My eyes darted around, first to the left where the bachelorettes seemed shaken but physically safe. With a sickening feeling I looked to my right and found Rocky curled into a ball and breathing too fast.

"Rocky," I whispered. "Breath slowly or you'll pass out. In with me and out like me," I told her until her breathing matched my own. Panic attack but otherwise okay.

I ignored the cries and whimpers behind me as bullets continued to fly and my gaze landed on Jana. Her long golden blonde hair was spread out on the floor but the rise and fall of her chest was off.

"Jana!" I crawled as quickly as I could without rising more than a few inches from the floor while the bullets continued to spray the shop, ruining everything in sight. "Jana, say something!"

"I..." that was it other than more gurgling sounds and my chest squeezed so tight I had to take a minute. Thankfully the bullets stopped and tires peeled away.

There was a long moment of silence before someone yelled. "Oh my God! What the fuck?" I didn't know who said that, only that her thoughts echoed pretty much everyone inside the Rainbow Canvas.

Jana coughed and that's when I saw it. The blood spurt out of her neck. It wasn't a good sign and in that moment I'd never been so grateful to my overbearing parents who insisted I go pre-med at Columbia, or for the time I spent working as an EMT in Panama and then in New York. It all came back to me as I watched Jana bleeding out at my knees. "Okay Jana save your energy. When I ask you a question, squeeze my hand. Once for yes and twice for no. Okay?"

One squeeze. Two.

CREATIVELY CRUSHED

"Perfect. Vision blurry?"

Two squeezes. No.

"Nausea?"

Another no.

"Pain?" She squeezed my hand as hard as she could and I had to blink back tears and move into action.

"Rocky, I need you to call 911." I issued orders while I removed my white tank top and applied pressure to Jana's neck while my other hand took her pulse at the wrist. "Tell them a pregnant woman, approximately twenty five weeks with a nicked artery. Shooter is off-site," I told her, suddenly back in New York stitching up wounds from knife fights and pimps with heavy fists, abused children and women. The worst of the worst and it had been my job to stitch them up just enough so they could go back out there and wreak more havoc.

I kept pressure on Jana's neck. "Just breath slowly, we need you calm so the baby is calm, okay? She will follow your lead Jana. She will." Her green eyes were still lucid, staring up at me afraid and trusting.

"Holy shit, Moon, who the hell are you?" Rocky looked up with wide, terrified eyes.

"Breathe, Rocky. I'm just me, good in an emergency." I'd had plenty of training and I knew I was capable, despite what people saw when they looked at me in my colorful flowing fabrics, bangles and fascination with all things non-traditional. "Someone open the door for the emergency workers."

"Got it," Rocky said, walking hesitantly to the door, gaze darting out the big broken window every other second until she was surrounded by police, fire and paramedics.

They swarmed my small shop but I couldn't focus on them and I couldn't answer their questions. Not now. Not with Jana rapidly losing blood. "Ma'am, please."

I looked at the two paramedics hunkering down next to me, their combined age younger than me. "I can't," I told them and impatiently explained the dilemma. "So get her on the damn gurney while I keep her alive."

"Yes ma'am," the blond one said and quickly they maneuvered around me and we practically ran out of the shop and to the ambulance. I stayed beside Jana the entire time, hand fused to her neck thanks to the white fabric between us, sticky with her blood.

The ride to the hospital was eternal, as in eternal hell because I knew what all the beeps meant, what the shouted stats meant and they all spelled out trouble. For Jana and her baby.

Rocky must have been busy on the phone because when we arrived at the hospital, crashing through the doors with me kneeling over Jana's nearly unconscious body, I saw several members of the Reckless Bastards motorcycle club staring at me with stunned expressions on their faces.

Max's in particular stayed with me, the anguish and worry on his rugged features was heartbreaking.

But I couldn't focus on them, I had to keep my hand where it was and focus on Jana.

She was a kind, brave soul. I knew the forces of the universe wouldn't let such a woman leave this world too soon. Jana and her baby would be safe.

They had to be.

Chapter Three

Cross

"Was that the art teacher?" I knew I sounded like an asshole but goddammit, this was just another damn complication.

"Her name is Moon," Max said with a deadly glare aimed at me. "And she's the reason my wife is still alive." His breathing was shallow and his nostrils flared, signs of a man in conflict.

"Why doesn't she just fucking let the paramedics do their goddamn job?" I was being an asshole, but I was worried for Max, and Moon was an easy target. She'd always seemed a little hippy dippy, which wasn't what I saw as she kept her hand on Jana's throat. She was serious and intense, kind of badass even. But I never would have pegged her for a glory hog.

"Who gives a shit? Jana has a chance!"

Goddammit, Max was right. Whatever the fuck had gone down at Moon's shop, it looked like she'd help save Jana. "You're right man. Need anything?"

"Just for my fucking wife to be okay," he grunted and began to pace in front of the windows. I just watched him, anger and fear radiating off him with every turn, every step.

I didn't know how long I sat there watching Max as more Reckless Bastards entered the waiting room, but it was long enough that they forced us to move up to the critical care waiting room. Finally, maybe an hour later, Rocky came in on shaky legs, looking pale and afraid.

Lasso was up and at her side in half a second, wrapping her in his arms. "How's Jana? Have you heard anything?" Her words were shaky and broken, projecting just how bad tonight had been.

"It was terrible, she was spurting and choking and I thought she was gonna die," Rocky gulped in a breath and clutched at Lasso's shirt. "But Moon was there, calm as can be as she issued orders and kept Jana calm.

CREATIVELY CRUSHED

She just whipped off her fucking shirt to stop the bleeding. Where is she?"

"Babe, settle down. We haven't heard anything yet. Have a seat." Lasso guided her to a chair and whispered in her ear until she was less frantic.

"How come we haven't heard anything yet?" Rocky blurted out.

"Exactly," Max growled. "Not one fucking word." He continued pacing, no doubt scaring all the doctors, nurses and family members who crossed his path.

"Any word yet?" Teddy asked as she showed up with her daughter, Quinn, in a stroller and a little black-haired boy holding her hand. The whole gang behind her, a parade of family – Mandy with Max and Jana's son Charlie and Gunnar's baby sister, Maisie.

"No," Max barked, getting angrier each time someone asked the question. I made a mental note to stop the next one.

"Tate's on his way," Teddy assured him from a distance, seeing he needed his space. It was always a trip to hear Teddy call Golden Boy by his given name, but she only did it to fuck with him.

More people arrived, more family. People I was responsible for keeping safe and I was doing a shitty job of it. Poor Jana didn't deserve this.

She'd already been through hell and back, never mind the hell she'd pulled Max from just in time. And Max, he looked ready to rip someone apart with his bare hands. Something had to be done, it just fucking had to be. I couldn't let more hurt and pain come to my club. My family. I got Jag on the phone. "Look up all the cameras near Rainbow Canvas and see what you can find."

"Done," he said, the one word clipped before the call ended.

The doors opened and every gaze in the waiting room turned to Moon, still shirtless and covered in blood, light eyes stunned and glassy. Her skirt hung to the floor, vibrant and beautiful in sharp contrast to the surroundings and events of the night. She went to Max and wrapped an arm around him, whispering to him as she led him away.

I was right behind them, listening to every word. "I'm sorry, Max. They assumed I was family and the doctor was out of the room before he finished his sentence. Do you want me to wait with you until the doctor returns?"

"I'll stay with him." Why I insisted on that, I had no fucking clue.

Moon nodded and stepped away, her eyes looking hurt and confused. Then more confusion as Max grabbed her arm. "No, stay. Did she say anything, Moon?"

Her lips twitched but I was too distracted by the bloody bra and killer set of tits on display as she crossed her arms.

"She did. Jana said to tell you not to do anything stupid. And to kick some ass." She rubbed Max's arm gently. "It's not good but she's going to pull through."

Max smiled but I could see how hard even that was for him. "Thanks, Moon." He took off his *kutte* and slid his t-shirt off over his head, handing it to Moon. "Here. Cover yourself up."

"Don't thank me, I'm just sorry it happened at all." She took his extra-large t-shirt and slipped it over her head. Moon wasn't like most of the women who interacted with the club. She wasn't intimidated by Max and didn't keep her distance. Seeing just how hurt my buddy was, she stepped in close and wrapped long, lean arms around him while Max cried his eyes out for his wife and unborn daughter. The sound was pure anguish and was like an arrow in my chest.

"Let it all out now, Max. Jana and Charlie are going to need that famous strength she's always going on and on about." His shoulders jerked like maybe he was laughing, and I stood watching, stunned by her gentle nature. "Besides, you might get to name the baby because she'll feel so bad about worrying you." She kissed his cheek and squeezed him into another tight hug that looked like pure comfort.

CREATIVELY CRUSHED

"Mr. Ellison," the doctor called out and Max went to him. Leaving me alone with Moon.

She walked over to me and said, "The shots came from a yellow and black sports car. It might have been a Mustang, I don't know. It looked like a Mustang, but it could have been any kind of sports cars with that style body."

Her words sank in and fire sparked in my veins as that tingle started in my extremities. Something was coming together, and soon I would have a piece of the puzzle.

"Thanks," I said gruffly and walked away before she noticed the half-chub I sported like a goddamn horny teenager.

Chapter Four

Moon

In the days after Jana was shot, I turned into a scared little girl, unable to leave the house beyond going to familiar places and only when necessary. I couldn't walk the fifty yards to my shop because I couldn't even think about what had happened there, the wreckage left behind. But I was a businesswoman and I couldn't simply let my fear and trauma keep me from taking care of business. After a quick glance at the clock on the wall, I called my insurance adjuster and an approved cleaning service who promised to meet me the day after tomorrow.

That meant I had forty-eight hours to get myself together. Centered and Zen enough to walk into my own shop. Like a professional.

Sleep had been another thing I couldn't do much of lately. Every time I closed my eyes all I could see was

Jana, gasping for breath like each one would be her last. My hands, coated in her blood. Even now I could see it when I washed my hands. I could still smell the metallic scent of that much blood. So much blood.

I couldn't sleep and I couldn't stop the guilt that this had happened when she was in my shop. The place that was meant to be warm and welcoming, a place where creativity was free to flourish. Now, it was something else.

"Are we visiting Jana today, Mom?" Beau looked up at me, his blue eyes shining behind his black glasses, curious and alert.

"Sure, but remember I told you she won't be awake." I'd been to visit Jana in the hospital at least once a day since this happened but explaining it to Beau was heartbreaking.

"She's in a coma," he said, now sad because he'd taken to Jana right away.

"That's right, but it's a medically induced coma so that she and the baby can heal faster."

CREATIVELY CRUSHED

"Do we have to go see Dr. Yang?"

I loved my little boy. At eight, he was too smart for his own good, perceptive and just incredible. But he did not like his regular visits to the lung specialist we'd been seeing for about two years. Chronic asthma that, despite everything we did to cure it, was as stubborn as I was.

"Yeah, Beau, we do. You know that."

"I know," he sighed, digging his toe into the kitchen linoleum. "But I'm breathing fine today. See?" Beau stood tall in his Pac-Man t-shirt and jeans because he had an aversion to shorts, and he sucked in several deep breaths before letting them out slowly so I could hear his lungs. "See, Mom?"

I knelt down so we were face to face, hands planted on his shoulders. "That's why we have to go in today, Beau. We have to make sure you're still doing well. It's just a precaution." He hated the speech, knew it by heart but he also knew I was right. His asthma problems were harder for me than they were for Beau because he had the luxury of hope, whereas I had the misfortune of a mother's worry. I had to listen to his chronic cough, his constant wheezing. Watch him sit on the sidelines instead of engage in the rough and tumble of the sports he loved. My eight-year-old powerhouse turned to books and science to corral his boundless energy.

"There's no reason to be scared," I promised to those wide eyes that always melted my heart. Even though I was terrified and no amount of yoga or meditation would help.

"What if it's worse, Mom? What if I can't go to school anymore?"

That was saying something since school wasn't Beau's favorite place. A kid with his smarts and his sensitivity was a target for most kids and my son seemed to attract them all.

"Then we'll find you the best tutor in the state and make sure you socialize in other ways." I couldn't help pulling him in for a hug and a kiss, his little boy scent reminding me why I worked so hard every single day.

CREATIVELY CRUSHED

And why I had to get back to the shop as soon as possible.

"It's my job to worry so let me do my job. Okay?"

He giggled and kissed me back. "Okay."

"Good. Let's get out of here." We piled into my car and battled Vegas traffic as we made our way to the larger hospital to see the respiratory specialist. Visiting Dr. Yang wasn't my favorite pastime either, but it was necessary. Essential.

We took x-rays and a breathing test, then waited. And waited. I counted the roses on the outdated wallpaper and fidgeted anxiously while Beau got lost in another one of his books. "Beau Vanderbilt," the nurse called and we went back to the office.

Dr. Yang was a forty something woman with silky black hair and kind eyes. "Good afternoon Beau, how are you feeling today?"

"Okay, Dr. Yang. How are you?"

She grinned affectionately. "Good, thanks for asking. So I have some news," she said to Beau though her gaze was fixed on mine.

"It's worse, isn't it?"

The doctor nodded, her eyes filled with sympathy. "The inflammation has worsened and your numbers are down I'm afraid, but not significantly. I think you'll find a nebulizer effective for handling your difficulty breathing. Could help with the inflammation in your airways, too."

Numb. That's how I felt. Listening to the doctors hadn't been a mistake but I should have listened to myself as well. "We'll get the nebulizer, but I'll also look into other, more natural treatments."

"That's fine. I'll do one treatment today so you can see how it's done and then you can do them at home. Three times a day to start."

"Three times a day? He has school and other activities." The one thing I never wanted for Beau was to have a childhood like mine, where he would be forced to act like a miniature adult at all times. I wanted him to be a kid. A normal kid. My parents had always been too concerned with appearances, so much so they denied me and my siblings a childhood.

"There are portable nebulizers that are battery operated. Just take it with you wherever you are." She gave a few more instructions while she administered the first treatment. "Pretty easy, right?"

Beau nodded. "It wasn't as bad as I thought."

"It never is," I assured him and helped him down from the exam table so we could get moving.

"Should we bring Jana's baby a toy?"

I smiled. "Sure buddy, let's stop at the gift shop."

Chapter Five

Cross

I fucking hated hospitals. The last time I was in one was when I said goodbye to my wife and child. It was the worst goddamn day of my life and showing up here every day only made it hurt more. Today there was another cause. A kid, maybe six or seven years old with inky black hair and big blue eyes hiding behind glasses with black frames way too stylish for someone so young. I'd watched him enter the waiting room and scan the whole place for a seat before he took the spot right beside me.

I held my breath, waiting for him to start talking my ear off about mundane kid things. It was mean as hell but being around kids was torture, always wondering if that was how old or how smart or funny my own kid would have been. But the kid pulled out a book and began to read.

Odd.

No matter how much I didn't want to be bothered, I couldn't just let a kid wander the hospital alone. "Hey kid, are you here alone?"

He looked up at me, blue eyes studying me carefully before he looked at my *kutte* and realized I was safe. "No. My Mom's visiting her friend who got hurt so I came out here to read. Mom said it was okay."

Smart kid. When women got together nothing good ever happened. "What's your name?"

"You can call me Beau," he said with a wide grin.

I smirked at how adult he sounded. "Is that your name?"

"No," he sighed, sounding annoyed as hell which amused me to no end. "It's Rainbeau, but kids are dumb and Mom said Beau is the name of a handsome man. You have a jacket like my friend, do you know him?"

CREATIVELY CRUSHED

I chuckled and rubbed my neck because Beau's questions came out like automatic fire. "What's your friend's name?"

"Max. Do you know him?"

"Yeah, but how do you know him?"

"He's married to my friend Jana. Why are you looking at me like that?"

He was right, I probably looked like I'd choked on something as the details slammed into place. The black hair was shorter and not quite as wavy. They didn't have the same eyes, hers were light green to his blue, but those rosebud lips and porcelain skin could only make him one person's child. "You're Moon's kid."

He nodded, a smile growing wide like I'd offered him free candy. "You know my Mom? She's the best, isn't she?"

She was something all right. "I do know her."

Beau frowned. "What's wrong?"

Great, the kid was as perceptive as his mother. "What makes you think something is wrong?"

"You have sad eyes and Mom says that eyes don't lie. What's the matter? Jana will be okay. The doctor said her vitals are strong. Hers and the baby's."

I blinked at his words, stunned by them. "You're pretty smart, eh?"

"I have a good memory," he announced with confidence but not the arrogance that often accompanied smarts. "Want me to read to you?"

"What are you reading?"

"It's about the cosmos and blackholes. You'll like it," he assured me as though it were already settled. But the truth was how did anyone say no to a kid so cute and so damn grownup?

"Sure, kid. That sounds nice."

"Cool," he said, scooting a bit closer so I could see the pictures. And then he settled down to read. Beau didn't play games or squirm or use his finger as a guide.

CREATIVELY CRUSHED

"You're a damn good reader, Beau."

"Well, duh, mister," he said with a proud grin. "I'm eight, you know.

"Eight, huh? And the name is Cross."

"I know, Mr. Cross. I'm small for my age. You don't have to tell me."

A shadow settled over us and the scent of jasmine and patchouli told me who the intruder was. Moon and she wore a floral print dress that showed off lean arms and sensual curves. Even now, all I could see was her in that bloody bra but looking sexy as hell. "Hey Beau, you're not bothering Cross are you?"

"No, he said I could read to him. Plus it's helping so he isn't sad anymore. About Jana," he clarified in his effort to keep me out of trouble, I assumed.

"I know, honey," she gave him a kind smile and ruffled his hair. "How are you, Cross?"

"Fine," I grunted out because I couldn't think of anything else. What was it about this woman, my polar opposite, who got me so tangled up that I said the wrong shit and usually ended up looking like a dick?

"Oooookay," she replied, giving me a cockeyed look. Then she stepped back and reached for her son. "Come on Beau, let's let Cross get back to his business. I gave Jana a hug for you and guess what?"

"What?"

"She squeezed back."

Beau went quiet and then he jumped out of his seat with a loud cheer. "Yes! That means she'll be awake soon."

I didn't know how in the hell the kid knew that, but I believed him. Watching Moon and Beau walk away filled me with a sadness and apprehension I couldn't understand. They were so happy, smiling while they talked about who knew what, completely oblivious to the world around them.

It looked nice.

It wasn't for me, but it was nice anyway.

CREATIVELY CRUSHED

***

"Hey man, pretty sure they have to be awake when you touch them like that."

Max looked up as I entered the room but his hand stayed wrapped around Jana's. "Cross. Hey."

"Hungry?"

"Not for cafeteria food," he grumbled and settled another worried gaze on his wife.

"Good thing. I don't fuck around with cafeteria food. Subs from Nitzki's Deli." I held up the bag filled with sandwiches, chips, and a heap of pickles.

"Thanks." He took the bag and dug in, reluctantly at first but then he let Jana's hand go and inhaled his lunch. "Damn, I needed that."

"Well I didn't need to see that shit. It was like watching a dinosaur eat." But a healthy appetite was a good sign, even for friends and family. "So how is she?"

"As good as we can expect, but honestly we don't know shit, not until she wakes up. She could be absolutely fine or she could be a damn vegetable. But the doctors say in another day or two she should begin to wake up on her own since they reduced her meds." Max scraped a hand over his face and groaned before settling his gaze on me. "What's up with you man, you look like shit."

"Don't worry about me, Max. I didn't come here to get into the shit with you, just checking on you both."

He grunted. "Might as well tell me since you need someone to talk to and I have no where else to be. Yet." I heard his words and I understood his meaning.

"It's just little shit that makes me feel like someone bigger than we know is out to get us. Fucking paper pushers complained about the width of the doors at Bungalow Three so we have to get them all expanded by a fucking eighth of an inch." They gave us thirty damn days or they'll shut us down. "Just stupid things. Cops tried to do a compliance check at one of the dispensaries too."

CREATIVELY CRUSHED

"What the fuck?"

"Exactly. Who else besides Roadkill would want us fucked up like this? It could be the Killer Aces, but I don't think so. This problem has to be local. We need to get Mayhem back under our control."

"You talk to the guys yet?" Max didn't wait for me to answer as his eyes widened. "That's what the barbecue was for wasn't it?"

"Yep. Great timing, right?"

"The best," he grinned, but it dimmed as he looked to Jana, pale and damn near lifeless in the bed.

"I have some other news." I didn't want to tell him but I owed him that much. If I was going to make up for what had happened to his wife, I had to start somewhere and this was as good a place as any. "You're not gonna like it but I need you to be cool."

"I'm listening." His tone said he wasn't listening at all, but I knew what I had to say would reel him in.

"Moon saw the car that fired into her shop. Yellow and black muscle car. She thinks it was a Mustang or something similar."

Max's jaws clenched and his eyes darkened with anger. No, not anger. It was fury. Blinding white fury.

"Fucking Vigo," he spat out, his thoughts mirroring my own. "I thought Buzzkill was supposed to take care of that asshole?"

"I thought so too. They had their chance, now it's open season."

"Damn right it is. I could use a bit of therapy right now," he said, smacking his palm with his fist.

"Yeah. Jag's looking into the footage around town just to be sure, but I have no fucking doubt it was him. But Max, and I mean the fuck out of this, don't worry about Vigo."

"How can I not?" He was angry and rightfully so, but I wouldn't budge on this.

"Because I'm your President and I'm telling you not to. Jana and Charlie and that little girl, they need you, man. They fucking need you to be here with them until they're out of trouble. And trust me, if you're not here and something does happen, you're done. You won't be able to forgive yourself and the fucking guilt will eat you alive."

"Cross," he began, understandably ready to fight. I didn't blame him. If there had been someone, anyone, to take out my anger on over Lauren's death, I would have. I would've been drunk off it, not stopping until the pain of losing her was gone.

It was never fucking gone. Not ever.

"I'm serious. When Jana wakes up, you better fucking be here. You and Jana are my family and Vigo is at the top of my list right now." That motherfucker had no idea how dead he already was. If he hadn't left Vegas yet, I'd make sure it was the decision he regretted most in his pathetic fucking life. "I got you."

Chapter Six

Moon

More than a week had passed since I set foot in my shop. It was the longest time I'd spent away since I opened it. Rainbow Canvas was my life and my only priority aside from Beau. Today, it needed all of my attention. Not for cleaning, because the insurance adjuster had already come out and done his part of the job and the window guys, painters for the outside and cleaners had done everything they could.

The state of the floors wrecked me, though. From the blood and the gunshots, I had to consider getting new floors or hiring a specialist to repair them because those floors used to be gorgeous and gave the shop personality. I could no longer look at the shop and see the place I created with hard work, love and a lot of elbow grease. Now it was foreign. Different. Strange. It was a crime scene.

And it felt like one, so I reached into the plastic bin behind the counter and grabbed a few bundles of sage and lavender and lit them at the entrance and the archway that led back to the painting area and gallery.

I sat on the floor as they burned, filling the air with relaxing, protective scents that settled my shoulders back to their normal position. I needed to clear my mind and center myself so that each time I looked at the spot at the right of the half circle, I didn't see Jana lying there bleeding out.

Thirty minutes later I was as stressed and worried as ever, and the sage and lavender had burnt out completely.

A knock sounded at the door that made me jump so high in the air, I was on my feet instead of my bottom. Looking out the window, I let out a groan at the sight of two detectives in ill-fitting suits. I stepped back so they could enter. "How can I help you, detectives?

The older one with the green eyes stepped in first.

CREATIVELY CRUSHED

"I'm Detective Haynes and this is Dodds. We're assigned to handle the shooting that took place last week." His eyes were kind but tired, like a man who had seen too much bad in the world to remain unaffected. "How are you doing, Ms. Vanderbilt?"

"It's hard being here but I'm okay. How can I help you gentlemen?"

The shorter one, Dodds stepped forward with an angry scowl on his face. "Why does it smell like marijuana in here?"

So he was going to be one of those cops. "Is that illegal in this state, detective?"

His frown deepened and he was even more in my face, not concerned with my height advantage because he had the gun. "Is that what I smell?"

"Actually, no. I haven't the faintest idea what you smell, Detective. Unless sage and lavender smell like pot, but if you have proof that it's what you think it is, I'm ready to hear it." When he said nothing I turned back to the nicer detective. "Did you come here to

59

arrest me for imagined crimes so you have an excuse not to solve the crime that actually took place here?"

"Not at all Ms. Vanderbilt." Detective Haynes flashed an annoyed look at his short, angry partner. "We just have a few questions about the night of the incident."

I didn't want to relive it but I wanted that psycho off the street. "Okay. Ask away, but he can't stay." I pointed to Dodds who thought he was being oh so clever, wandering around the shop in hopes to find some pot lying around. As if I would ever be that careless.

"That's not your choice," he said from the back and I didn't bother turning my head, because I knew where he was standing.

"Well if that's the case then I'd prefer not to speak to the police until I've spoken to a lawyer." I knew how people saw me because I made sure they saw me that way. It was an attempt to leave the old me behind, the girl who wasn't Moonbeam and who wouldn't be caught dead in cheap non-designer brands. People like

CREATIVELY CRUSHED

Detective Dodds weren't worth my time or effort, guys who didn't bother to look below the surface or consider that outside packaging gave no indication of what was inside. But just because I looked like a pot smoking hippie, didn't mean I was one. I was, but I was also raised by wealthy and powerful parents, which meant I knew my rights and the power of an attorney.

"We're trying to help you, lady," the little man said.

"I think your captain will love to know how you treat crime victims, detective. Maybe you need more time at the academy so you can learn to be something other than a total ass." His aura was toxic and that told me everything I needed to know about the man. He was poison.

He leaned forward as he drew closer, trying to intimidate me. "What did you call me?"

"Is your hearing defective as well?"

He glared, face so red I thought he might keel over and die right in my shop which would just be unfortunate. "I could arrest you."

"Dodds! Get out of here goddammit." Haynes looked to be at the end of his rope as he stared down his tiny partner who huffed and puffed before finally exiting my shop. "Sorry about that, Ms. Vanderbilt. Let's just say that he's my punishment for a past sin."

"No apology necessary. At least you acknowledge that he's a crappy cop."

"Ms. Vanderbilt," he began on an exhausted sigh.

"Call me Moon, please." Reminding me of my family was not the way to inspire me to be helpful.

"Moon, just remember that no good deed goes unpunished."

As if I hadn't learned that truism too many times to count in my life. "Believe me, I know but this isn't a good deed. I'll tell you the same thing I told the uniforms who showed up the night of the incident. There was a yellow sports car, yellow and black actually. It looked like the car from Transformers," I told him nervously, explaining when his brows rose. "My son owns one of those models, it's his favorite."

He smirked. "What about the shooter, did you see anything? Race? Hair color or eye color?"

My head was already shaking in response. "No, there was no skin on display just a mass of blackness that I assumed meant he or she was wearing gloves. Just darkness and then a flash of light when the gun went off." Even replaying it my mind had my breath racing and shallow. My skin began to heat, and my hands started to shake but I could always count on deep breathing exercises. They never failed me. "That's all I saw, Detective Haynes, I'm sorry."

He scribbled in his miniature notepad for a long time before he closed it and looked up with a grin. "You were pretty handy to have around, especially for Mrs. Ellison."

I nodded at his words, hearing the next question before he even asked it. "In another life I was an EMT."

"And how well do you know Mrs. Ellison?"

"The victim?" I asked for clarification because again, these cops weren't as clever as they liked to think. "Well enough to know that CPA's don't often draw that kind of client dissatisfaction, detective." He grimaced but had the grace to look ashamed. A little.

"I'm just trying to help, Moon, and that means figuring out who did this."

"No, you *assume* that this has something to do with her husband's motorcycle club. It might or it might not, but knowing the color of a car doesn't tell you that unless I've missed some new investigative techniques?"

He smiled but it was one of frustration and restraint. "It's a safe bet though, isn't it?"

"I don't know detective, what about the incident a few months ago that involved that Governor? That had nothing to do with the club, did it?"

He sighed because I was adding to his exhaustion but he could join the club. I'd been exhausted for years with no end in sight so his was none of my concern. "Okay, it didn't. Happy?"

"No I'm not happy. Someone shot up my business and my friend is still in the hospital. Happy is the last thing I'm feeling. Look, Jana and Max both came here for my painting classes and that's how I met them. Jana and I became friends and that's all I have for you."

"Thanks. If you can think of anything else, please let me know." Detective Haynes left his card on the glass checkout counter and left, taking his toxic little partner with him.

Dealing with the police was never my favorite thing, not since I'd seen up close just how they treated those entrusted in their care. Thanks to my family's money and my privilege, I only found myself on the wrong side of them once. I wouldn't forget it. Ever.

Another knock sounded and I practically jumped out of my skin. I wasn't in the mood for visitors and I was much too jumpy to deal with customers or artists at the moment. But I was clearly visible from the window so I looked up and frowned, walking to the door and unlocking it again. "Cross. What are you doing here?"

He stood in the doorway, so big and imposing that I would have felt intimidated by him if he'd ever given me a reason to fear him. Cross might be surly but he didn't seem to be dangerous. To me anyway. Hands shoved in his pocket, he looked a little scared. "I came to apologize for the other day. I was out of line and rude for no reason, and I'm sorry about that."

I stepped back so he could come into the shop and locked the door behind him. Given the events of the last few weeks it didn't matter much but it made me feel safer. Or something. "It's fine, Cross, really. You don't have to like me, especially since you haven't done much to make yourself all that likable."

He smirked and crossed his arms, giving me a long glimpse of the tattoos covering his forearms. Blue eyes sparkled with something akin to mischief and I swear to Mother Earth, the tiny smile transformed his whole face from angry curmudgeon to holy smokes irresistible bad boy. "You don't find me likable?"

CREATIVELY CRUSHED

"You're plenty likable," I told him as I worked hard to tamp down the desire that welled up at that smile. "Until you open your mouth." He really was entirely too good looking with his tall frame and wide shoulders, thick brown hair that looked like it belonged in a shampoo commercial and eyes so blue they could rival the ocean. He was as handsome as he was dangerous, but it was the latter I needed to remember.

"There may be some truth to that," he admitted sheepishly. "What's that smell?"

"Sage and lavender. To get rid of the bad energy in this place." I knew he would think it was some type of voodoo or hocus pocus, or whatever other phrase people used to describe things they couldn't understand.

"Smells good. Kind of like pot."

I scoffed. "Now you sound like Dodds."

"That guy's a fucking dick."

"Agreed." I looked around the shop one final time and sighed. Everything looked normal and in time, I was sure it would feel normal as well. Hopefully. "Thank you for stopping by Cross but the apology wasn't necessary."

"It was. I don't dislike you, Moon." He shoved his hands into his pockets and rocked on his heels, the same way Beau did when he wanted to ask for something he knew he couldn't have.

"It's okay if you do." It took me a long time to become comfortable with that but being me felt better than being accepted for being someone else.

"I don't. Can I walk you home?"

I smirked but nodded at the gesture. It was nice and kind of old school. I liked it. "Sure. But, I live right here." I gestured to the side of the building. I locked up and Cross fell into step beside me. Quietly. "How are you doing, Cross?"

"Fine," he said quickly.

"Okay. But how are you really?" I stopped and put a hand to his chest. "Humor me."

CREATIVELY CRUSHED

Those blue eyes stared at me for a long time but there was no hate or malice or even mild dislike in them. There was bone deep fatigue, concern and a fear in them I was sure he'd rather die than let me see. He started walking and I figured the conversation was over and fell in step beside him. "I'm tired as hell, Moon."

I felt myself softening towards his honesty. "That wasn't so hard was it? Are you having trouble sleeping?"

"No trouble because I just gave up trying to sleep." His words were harsh and sardonic.

My heart went out to him. I didn't know much about the Reckless Bastards but I knew they were a motorcycle club and I knew they had plenty of business interests around town. I also knew the cops thought they were criminals and that bad luck seemed to follow them. "Doesn't your club own a few dispensaries, because I'm pretty sure pot is a good sleep aid."

Thick chocolate brows arched. "You toke up, Moon?"

I smiled and shook my head. "Not anymore. When I partake, it's strictly edibles because of Beau's asthma. In fact, do you have some time right now?"

He frowned. "For what?"

We stood in front of my house and I climbed the steps. "Therapy and you won't even have to talk about your feelings." He grinned and climbed the steps, shaking his head.

"How can I pass up an offer like that?"

***

What on earth possessed me to invite Cross into my home? The man was hurting and he clearly couldn't express any vulnerability to his club, or probably anyone else. If I could help him, I would. But I refused to get involved. "Come on in and take off your shoes and that vest."

"Is that necessary?"

CREATIVELY CRUSHED

I turned to face him, hands on my hips the way I did when Beau decided to question my decisions. "Yes."

And that was all it took to get him to oblige. He kicked off his heavy duty boots and hung the leather vest with the Reckless Bastards insignia on one of the hooks beside the door. "Happy?"

"No. Satisfied. Now come and have a seat." The squeak of his much heavier frame easing into the cushion sounded as I went to retrieve what I needed to help him.

"I made these," I told him and stopped when I returned and saw him stretched out on the sofa with his eyes half closed. He looked peaceful and I didn't want to rouse him.

"I'm not asleep. Yet," he said and sat up. "What the hell kind of air freshener do you use?" He sounded grumpy about it and that made me laugh.

"It varies from week to week. Different scents that instill calm and relaxation. Too much stress can be bad for Beau."

He smiled. "Where is he?"

"Hanging out with Rocky. I don't know if it's her red hair or that slight hint of southern twang I hear in her voice, but Beau is absolutely taken with her."

"He's a cool kid. Very, ah, adult."

I laughed and set down the two containers. "He's mature for his age, I know."

"I like it. I'm not really the baby talk kind of guy," he said gruffly, seeming uncomfortable as I sat on the coffee table directly in front of him.

"No kidding. It would probably freak him out if you did." I'd never treated Beau like a baby because he was too smart for me to get away with it and because I couldn't afford to baby him during his early years. But when his asthma got out of control I did worse than baby him, I became a mother hen. "I have hemp oil and

CREATIVELY CRUSHED

CBD cream. I made them both and I'm going to combine them. All you have to do is relax."

Cross looked skeptical but he nodded and I took one of his big hands into both of mine and began massaging his hand and wrist. It took a few minutes, but as soon as he stopped resisting me, Cross began to relax. The weight of his big body sank deeper into the sofa just as I knew it would. Every inch of him was rock hard and not just his muscles, but the knots of tension. "Damn that feels good."

I smiled and switched to his other hand, feeling a smug sense of satisfaction when his arm remained limp. His hands were big and calloused, like he worked with his hands, which made me curious. "What exactly do you *do*?"

He opened one eye and stared at me. "Seriously?"

I nodded, adding more pressure to his palm and pulling a groan from him. "Yes, seriously. If you don't want to answer, don't." I never understood why people were so secretive, especially in this digital age. With a credit card and a wi-fi connection I could have his life story in under an hour.

"I'm the President of the Reckless Bastards which basically puts me as CEO of our business interests."

"Interesting." I'd never thought about the club like an actual, official organization or corporation but it made sense. The truth was I didn't think all that much about the club because I didn't want to know. But I wanted to know about Cross.

"Yeah? Why?"

I shrugged and stood in front of him, noticing the way he made a gentlemen's effort to avoid looking at my chest. I urged him to stretch out again and stood behind him so I could get to work, my hands on the side of his head.

"Because I never thought of it like that. Jana's mentioned casually about the dispensaries, the gun shop and even a brothel or two but I guess I just assumed...actually I don't think I assumed anything. It's pretty cool that you're a CEO."

CREATIVELY CRUSHED

I'd started working on a pressure point.

He grinned. "These days it doesn't feel all that cool," he said honestly and I knew he was feeling relaxed. "Oh, shit, Moon."

The sound that came from the back of his throat was downright sensual, like the sound a man makes when he first slides into a moan. Satisfied but hungry for more. And all I was doing was massaging his temples. His hands floated back like a baby's, fingertips brushing the sides of my arms as if I wasn't already too aware of him.

"Holy shit." His hands gripped my wrists as my fingertips lightly pressed into his head.

I ignored his touch and the heat it sent through me and kept going because Cross needed this. He would never admit it, at least not to me, but he didn't have to. "Relax, Cross."

"I am."

"Relax completely. Hands too, down at your sides. It's more effective, trust me." Not that he owed me trust but since I had his head in my hands, he didn't have a choice.

"Sorry."

"It's fine. Relax." He finally did and I was able to focus, sliding my fingers down the back of his head to his shoulders which were as hard as granite. The man carried his stress everywhere and there was a lot of it.

"Moon," he groaned again and I felt my nipples harden and I just hoped he couldn't see the effect that deep, gravelly voice was having on me. "Fuck."

I gave him at least five solid minutes on each of his shoulders until every lump and knot was gone. He was practically boneless when I stepped back with a satisfied smile. "Better?"

"Hell yeah. Thank you, Moon."

"I'm just glad I could help." I wasn't expecting anything from Cross, but the fact that I could help another hurting soul, even temporarily, meant something to me.

CREATIVELY CRUSHED

"Where'd you learn all this anyway? Massage expert? Medical professional? What's next? Ninja?"

A laugh spilled out of me at his words. "Ninja? I wish. Despite the graceful woman you see before you, I am the exact opposite of a ninja."

"But?" He looked up at me, a mischievous grin lighting up his face.

"I used to be an EMT when I lived on the east coast and then later I got into alternative and holistic medicine."

"Because of Beau?"

He was perceptive. "I already had an interest, but it kind of went into overdrive after his asthma worsened."

"Nothing wrong with protecting your kid. It's your job." He said it with such conviction I knew there was a story there but now wasn't the time.

"Agreed." I stepped around to put some distance between us, until the intimate little bubble we'd found ourselves in quietly burst. "I have some things I need to take care of," I told him and pushed at his shoulders when he tried to stand. "But you should take fifteen or twenty minutes to lie there and relax. And then you can leave and ruin all of my hard work with your stressful life."

He smiled a half-smile, looking so handsome I had to look away. "Thanks Moon."

"I'm glad I could help. Take care of yourself, Cross." Even though we weren't actually friends and barely even acquaintances despite how many times we'd crossed paths over the past few years, I really hoped he'd take care of himself.

Chapter Seven

Cross

Spending time with Moon had been unexpected but nice. I thought I'd just stop by her shop and offer up an apology, which she would give me a hard time about, and then be on my way. But Moon wasn't just some flighty hippie chick, she was a good woman with a good heart. Even though I'd seen the heat in her eyes more than once in the hour I'd spent with her, she'd never made a move or even flirted with me.

Hell, I was pretty sure a few times she was treating me like her kid and instead of pissing me off, it amused me. Fucking amused me, which I didn't even think was possible anymore.

I left her place feeling more relaxed than I had in a long damn time. As I rode back to the clubhouse, I thought about how I'd never been more grateful for someone to touch me. The pain in my neck and shoulders was gone. My head felt clear, I was focused.

Her hands were fucking magic. I hadn't felt this good in years. Well, since Lauren, anyway.

When I pulled up to the clubhouse there was a white fucking station wagon with a Mayhem city logo on the front door.

What the fuck were the fucking paper pushers doing here now?

Since the clubhouse was not a public place I knew exactly where they were. The shooting range. My motorcycle boots were the only sound aside from the blood rushing through my head as I came closer and closer to our pride and joy. We sank a lot of money into RB Gun Range but we'd more than made it back over the years because despite the crazies, Americans loved us some guns.

"What's going on in here?"

A short round man with curly black hair turned to me, brown eyes flashing fear before he remembered who the fuck he was. "City Inspector," he said and flashed a badge too fast for me to see. "We have a few issues here, Mr. Wylie."

"I need to see that ID."

He stared with a smirk on his face until he realized I wasn't joking. "You don't want to make this harder than it needs to be."

"By asking you to identify yourself? Funny, I thought that was the law." He handed me the badge and I stared at it for a long time, snapping an image with my phone before handing it back. "What problems have you found, Stuart?"

He swallowed. "There's no clear indicator where your bullets are being deposited once discharged."

More fucking bullshit. "Are you with the EPA or the City?"

Stuart swallowed again and removed a kerchief from his pocket. "The City as my identification states."

"And the City has been authorized to enforce federal regulations? Hang on so I can get my lawyer on the phone." These guys were full of shit, once again, and I was damned tired of it.

I stared him down as I waited for my call to go through.

"Cross, what can I do for you?" Tanya was a boisterous blonde from Georgia, but she was a damn good lawyer who didn't take shit and had no problem working for an MC.

I gave her a quick rundown of Stuart's claims. "What should I do?"

"Whatever you do, don't kick his sniveling fucking face in or you'll have trouble. Just take the paperwork and make sure it's dated and signed. Make sure everything is laid out and easy to understand. When that shithead leaves, send it to me and I'll take care of it."

I breathed a sigh of relief. "Thanks Tanya."

"It's why y'all pay me the big bucks." She laughed and ended the call before I could.

CREATIVELY CRUSHED

I slid the phone back into my back pocket and stared at Stuart, fighting the urge to ignore Tanya's warning and pummel his face. That thought just pissed me off because it reminded me of Moon's words before I drifted off on her sofa. *And then you can leave and ruin all of my hard work with your stressful life.* "Well?"

"There is another matter. The guns, do you have proof they were purchased legally?"

"Are you fucking kidding me?"

He shook his head while wiping more sweat from his forehead and his brow. "I assure you I am not."

"Right. Then show me what law says I have to."

"Look, there's no reason to—"

"Show me the goddamn paperwork or get the fuck off my property, Stuart."

With quick moves, Stuart scribbled on a sheet of paper and handed it to me. "You have fourteen business days to answer our requests or fines will incur."

"You done?" He opened his mouth to say more but my patience was done. "Get the fuck out." I didn't raise my voice because I didn't need to, Stuart got the message and got out of my sight real fucking fast.

Even with him gone, my anger and frustration hadn't subsided. Despite all of Moon's work to calm me down, which had worked dammit, I was all riled up again. My mind raced to connect the dots. I knew all the bullshit the Bastards were going through with the city was connected even if I didn't know how. Or why they'd targeted the Reckless Bastards. But I knew who would and I called him as I headed back to my bike.

"What's up, Cross?"

"Jag, can you do a deep dive to see who we pissed off in city government? I can't figure out all the pieces yet, but a city inspector was just at the gun range."

He whistled. "Two weeks ago it was Bungalow Three."

"And I'm sure more will come. Can you do it?"

CREATIVELY CRUSHED

"Sure. Not like I got shit else to do. I'll let you know when I have something." And then the call was over, making me question my leadership skills again.

I couldn't think of any of that, not right now, when I was so damn desperate to reclaim the calm I felt before I got back to the clubhouse. How could the one place that mattered to me the most, be the biggest source of my stress?

That was another question I couldn't—or wouldn't—answer, not now. I needed something else to focus on and as I passed one of the three titty bars in Mayhem, I found the perfect fucking thing. A yellow and black Camaro that someone who didn't know cars would mistake for a Mustang, and it was sticking out like a sore thumb. "Perfect."

I wouldn't do anything tonight. Probably. But I did wander into the club like I owned it. Not that anybody noticed, which was fine with me.

My goal was to follow Vigo, let him know that I had my eye on him. If White Boy Craig was happy to look like a punk ass bitch and let this snitch live, he didn't deserve the respect of me not killing this fuckwad as soon as I got the chance. *Not tonight,* I had to remind myself at least a dozen times as I watched him sitting right up front and making lewd comments to the dancers. Cheap fucker tossed out dollar bills and then got angry when the girls found bigger pockets to dance for.

"All that money you got for selling out your club and you're handing out singles? Pathetic."

He froze, and his face went pale as I stood beside him. Too close. "Yeah? What are you gonna do about it?"

I smiled. "Right now? Nothing. But soon, Vigo. That's a fucking promise." I left a bullet, a hollow point, on the table in front of him and walked away. Let that asshole stew over that. It didn't take long for him to get spooked. About ten minutes later he slid into that yellow eyesore and hit the road with me right on his ass.

He stopped at a whorehouse—not one of ours—but it took him fifteen minutes before he was walking out again with a satisfied smirk on his face. Because it took a real man to please a woman being paid to fuck you, right? I followed Vigo all night. Everywhere he went I was like his fucking shadow. He stopped at a biker bar and I was there at the other end of the bar watching.

Then a rundown apartment building where he was greeted by a woman with chunky red and blonde highlights. He went inside with the woman and did who knew what, but the lights stayed on for a few hours before all signs indicated they were in for the night.

I wouldn't be fooled so easily and since I couldn't sleep and had nothing else going on, I waited. And waited. Finally, four hours later, that smarmy shit heel walked out and I followed him because he was out of places to go. He couldn't go to Roadkill even if he wanted to, not with them looking to kill his ass and he'd gone everywhere else he could.

"You're out of options," I muttered while he idled at a four-way stop sign trying to figure out if he could out-maneuver me. He'd spotted me in his rear view by now.

We both knew he couldn't get away from my bike and he finally, slowly made a right turn. Then a left before hooking another right into a parking lot that sat in front of a small four-story apartment building that looked like it was built in the sixties. He scanned the parking lot and when his gaze landed on mine, I flipped him off.

"Asshole!"

That only made me grin. I waited until he went inside before I got off my bike and walked the same path Vigo had until I was outside his door. I balled a fist and pounded the door in two sharp knocks. "Time's running out, Vigo."

And then I went home and slept for at least one full hour.

It wasn't much but it was progress.

***

CREATIVELY CRUSHED

I pulled up to Moon's house with a big smile on my face. The reason? About fifty pounds of nearsighted, adorable goofiness standing just inside the front porch.

"Hi, Cross, did you come to read with me again?" Beau looked up as he pushed his glasses up his nose, his mouth pulled into a wide grin.

"Hey, little man. Rocky asked me to bring some paintings to your mom." Why I'd let the little spitfire talk me into it, I didn't know. Okay, that was a damn lie, I knew why. For some reason I found Moon's presence more soothing than annoying now that I knew her better.

"I like Rocky." He flashed another grin that was so damn contagious my lips were already pulling into a matching grin. "We painted Monster Trucks the other day. Hang on, I'll tell Mom you're here."

The sound of his feet shuffling across the floor cut through the quiet house and I wondered where exactly Moon was hiding.

"Come in," he said when he came back, unlocking the screen door to let me in.

"Is she busy?"

"Just finishing yoga so you have to wait."

I set the paintings down against the wall underneath a window and took the same seat I'd had on my last visit. I noticed the wheeze in his voice that Moon had talked about but didn't know if I should mention it, so I just said, "What's up, Beau?"

"Not much. I got new asthma meds but I don't like them."

"No one likes medicine, kid. We endure it because we don't want to stay sick."

"It's not getting better. It's getting worse and Mom is scared even if she says she's not." He pouted which was so strange when he sounded so grownup.

CREATIVELY CRUSHED

"Parents are always scared, it's part of their job. You'll be fifty and she'll still worry about you like you're five." I stood, feeling uncomfortable talking to a kid about such personal things. Beau took in a deep breath and the wheeze intensified, giving me a taste of the anxiety Moon lived with. Shit. No kid should have to fight for air.

And then I was struck dumb. Mute. Paralyzed by the sight of Moon in skintight purple, her body contorted erotically. Just a sliver of a view into the patio as we walked by the living room and me unable to look away. Who knew yoga was so sensual?

"Want some cereal? Mom made it yesterday." Beau was already headed to the kitchen, leaving me no choice but to follow him.

"She *made* cereal?"

"Yep. It has less fake sugar but it's still really good." He pulled out two brightly colored bowls and poured from a clear plastic container. When he grabbed the milk, I stepped in.

"Maybe I should pour the milk," I told him and his skin turned bright red.

"Okay but Mom doesn't care if I spill, she says people spill stuff all the time. That's why kitchens are full of towels."

"Hey Cross." Moon breezed in still wearing her sexy purple getup, skin glistening and slightly pink from the sun. And the yoga. "Did we have a meeting today?"

"Nope." I stared at her and she stared back, waiting for me to say more.

"Rocky asked him to drop off art," Beau said, selling me out and pointing to the paintings in the living room.

I shoved a bite of cereal in my mouth and grinned. "Yeah, that."

She smirked and dipped her head in the fridge, giving me a side view of the curve of her ass. It was as magnificent as I expected. "How do you like the cereal?"

CREATIVELY CRUSHED

I blinked at her change of subject. "Really good. You made this?"

"With my own hands," she held them up and then took a long sip of water from a glass she had chilling in the refrigerator. "How are you?" The question was benign enough but the look in those green eyes said she knew all of my secrets, even the ones no one knew.

"Fine. Still tired."

She sighed and did that sympathetic head tilt thing women were born knowing how to do. "Too bad. If you ever want to do yoga with me, the offer stands." I opened my mouth to answer and she put up a hand to stop me. "Just think about it and if you decide to do it, just let me know."

I nodded but her look said she knew I wouldn't take her up on her offer and for that reason alone, I was seriously considering it.

"And how are you?" I asked to change the subject.

Her gaze slid down to Beau who was already deep in a book that I hadn't even seen him retrieve.

"Working on being okay. Doing a lot of meditation and waiting for the medication to kick in." Her lips quirked into a smile as she ruffled her son's hair.

We fell into that seven-second lull thing and I searched for something to say. "Need some help with the paintings?"

Her gaze shot to the paintings leaning against the wall and I saw the fear in her gaze a moment before she banked the look and shook her head. "Nah, I'll take them when I go over to the shop. Later."

"You sure?" She nodded and wiped some of the sweat gathering at the base of her throat.

"Want to stay for lunch?"

Beau looked up and smiled. "Yeah! We're having chickpea burgers!"

That sounded awful but the company was the best offer I'd had in a long damn time. "I love burgers."

"Me too! And Mom makes the best fries ever!"

Moon blushed prettily. "Ever?"

CREATIVELY CRUSHED

Beau nodded. "Yep! Even better than *Carina's*!"

"It's an organic restaurant," she explained and I was in awe of Moon, going above and beyond to make sure her boy had the best life possible even with his limitations.

"It's our favorite," he said, smiling at me like we shared a secret. "Mom, we should take Cross, he'd like it. I know it!"

The kid was probably right but Moon gave him the answer hated by kids around the world. "We'll see, honey."

Unlike most kids, Beau nodded. "Okay." Then he looked to me again with mischief in his eyes. "Can I ride on your motorcycle?"

I had no fucking clue what to say to that, but I knew enough from Jana, Rocky and Teddy to know that if I looked to Moon it would mean no so, I kept my gaze glued to his.

Then I shoved a heaping spoon of cereal into my mouth.

Chapter Eight

Moon

"Oh Jana, I came as soon as I heard!" An immense sense of relief washed over me as Jana's big eyes stared up at me from her hospital bed. Emotions warred within me but I resisted the urge to pull her into my grasp and hug her with all my might. "I'm so happy to see you awake."

She smiled at me and reached for my hand. "Moon. Thank you." The tight squeeze told me she was thanking me for more than being here today. "You saved my life," she said, her voice suddenly watery and I couldn't hold my own emotions inside any longer.

Tears fell down my cheek as I looked at the monitors beside the bed. "You and the baby seem to be doing much better. How do you feel?"

"Like I'm ready to get the hell outta here. But now that I'm awake they want to poke and prod me until I go nuts and they get to lock me up in the crazy palace." She smiled but the smudges under her eyes told me just how much of a toll this had taken on her.

"You'll be home soon enough and your big strapping husband will wrap you in cotton until the baby is born."

Jana laughed. "If he has his way he'll swaddle me in it forever."

"He must be so relieved. Although I think the nurses and doctors are more relieved," I told her, explaining what a bear he'd been when we first arrived at the hospital. "Even the guys kept their distance," I told her, never really sure what to call the Reckless Bastards. Calling them club members sounded too country club for those tough guys but saying *the gang* might make people draw the wrong conclusions, so I stuck with the all-encompassing *guys*.

Jana reached out for me again and I stepped closer, leaning against the side of the sturdy hospital bed to make things easier for her. "He told me that you held him while he cried, Moon. Thank you. He's been doing great, but he could've gone down a dark path if you hadn't offered your special brand of comfort. I'm just thanking you all over the place." More tears fell and she cried harder as I comforted her.

I laughed nervously, uncomfortable with her praise. "I don't need any thanks, Jana. You're my friend and I did what friends do."

She snorted. "I couldn't have done what you did, no matter how much I might want to. Rocky thinks you're a secret agent."

That pulled a laugh from me. "Well she was pretty shaken up so her perspective is a little off."

"Don't believe her, Jana. She's a total badass!" Rocky strolled in with her baby on her hip and Beau at her side. "Hey babe," she said and gave me a one arm hug.

"Jana, hi!" Beau stood on the other side of the bed with a wide grin. He was close but not too close since he'd been given plenty of warnings that she was in pain. "How are you?"

"Better now that my buddy is here." She reached out and tugged him close for a half hug. "Thanks for visiting me. How are you doing, Beau?"

"I'm better now that you're awake. I missed you." He gave her hand a squeeze and then settled into a chair with his book.

I visited with Jana for a bit longer before plenty of other well-wishers showed up. The room got too crowded, so Beau and I headed home for some quiet time before dinner in a few hours.

"Mom," he asked in a voice too worried for a little boy. "Will Jana be good as new?"

"Yep. The doctor says she and her baby will be perfectly fine." And that was the best news I'd gotten all week. Things were finally returning to normal, mostly. The shop had reopened and things were fine. Everyone had come back to show their support, but it was only Wednesday. The truth would be revealed on Friday night. I wondered if the gunfire scared away the Friday night crowd permanently.

CREATIVELY CRUSHED

"Mom?"

Already on alert by his tone, I slid a gaze to Beau who had a red face and his chest was heaving. Shallow breathing followed by a wheezing inhale, and I knew he was on the verge of another asthma attack.

"Hang on, honey!" My sandaled foot hit the gas and I sped the rest of the way home because like an idiot, I'd left the batteries for the portable nebulizer on the charger. At home.

Minutes later I had my son in my arms, struggling to carry him into the house with only one thought in my mind. *Get him to the nebulizer.*

Beau's room was upstairs, across the hall from mine. I managed to get him into his bedroom, nearly as out of breath as he was before I laid him on his bed with the Milky Way bedspread and began setting up the machine and the medicine.

"Stay calm, Beau. Just a moment." I inhaled deeply and exhaled deeply until Beau followed along.

"It's. Okay. Ma. Ma. Mom."

That wheezing sound broke my heart. It wasn't okay, none of this was okay. Beau was a sweet little boy who didn't deserve this terrible problem. If I could, I would take on this burden for him. I put the mouthpiece between his lips. "Okay, now breathe."

He inhaled deeply several times before his body began to relax. His eyelids slowly slid down, a sure sign that he was feeling better. His attacks were never easy for me either. They drained my energy for the rest of the day. I'd read all about *status asthmaticus*. Every day I worried that one of his asthma attacks would be fatal.

His eyes were shut and his breathing had returned to normal, slow and steady even though it was still a bit wheezy. I brushed his hair from his face and pressed a kiss to his forehead.

Now it was time to meditate. I needed to relax. Get my good juju back.

If I was being honest, meditation hadn't been working this past week. I constantly felt on edge and no matter how much I meditated, communed with nature and tried to instill inner peace, nothing worked. Not even my pot-laced homemade granola. Or cornbread. There was something in the air; it crackled with electricity and tension. I didn't know what was up, but I knew it was about to change everything.

Everything.

Trudging downstairs, heavy with fatigue, I was brought up short by the man standing in the middle of my living room. Scowling at me.

"Cross, what are you doing here?"

"A better question is why in the hell is your door wide open?"

While I appreciated his protectiveness, I did not appreciate his tone. "What business is it of yours? Do you always just walk into people's houses without an invitation and yell at them?"

"The open door was the goddamn invitation! What if I was the asshole in the yellow and black car?"

I hated that he went there because the same thought had just flashed in my mind. "We both know he wasn't looking for me."

"It doesn't matter. You can't leave your door wide open like that, Moon!"

I sighed and dropped down on the sofa, exhausted. "You don't think I know that, Cross? It's not a habit."

"Good, because it'd be a pretty fucking stupid one!"

He was testing my patience and I'd worked hard to keep it in check over the years. I couldn't believe I was almost in tears. "Well next time my son is in the middle of an asthma attack, I'll stop to lock the door so Cross doesn't get all bent out of shape."

He sucked in a breath. "I'm sorry. Is Beau all right?"

"He's fine. I did the breathing treatment right away and now he's fast asleep." I pinched the place on my nose between my eyes, willing the tears not to fall.

CREATIVELY CRUSHED

"Good," he said on a sigh and dropped down beside me. "How are you holding up?"

"Really? I'm not. His attack terrified the hell out of me and then some big bad biker came in my house and yelled at me."

"Shit, I'm sorry to make things worse but…hell I've just been so worried lately."

"Welcome to my world." I took a deep breath. I didn't want him to see me crying, see me weak. I was supposed to be Zen. Calm. Collected. "Want to meditate with me?" My question shocked him but he masked it quickly.

"I don't know, do I?"

A laugh escaped me and I stood, nodding my head for him to follow. "Come on." I felt his presence behind me and I willed my body not to react to his nearness. "We won't do a full on meditation, just some breathing techniques."

"Breathing? Sounds like yoga to me. Are you going to put on that badass purple outfit?" His skepticism wasn't surprising, but it amused me.

I smiled. "Come on and sit down." I led him out to the backyard but not before locking the front door. "Cross your legs and close your eyes. Now just relax and focus on your breathing. Listen to your breathing and nothing else."

"Not even you?"

My lips curled up in a smile. "Just listen and focus on your breathing, keeping it even. Let it mimic mine." I took in several deep breaths through my nose for a count of eight and let it out slowly, focusing on the air as it left my mouth. I could hear Cross at my side, his breathing a beat behind my own.

Soon the only sound besides the crickets was our breathing, mingling together until slowly the worry of the day faded away. There were still plenty of other worries to keep me down but for now I was determined to let the tension and the stress fade away.

CREATIVELY CRUSHED

Inhale.

Exhale.

Inhale.

Exhale.

On the next inhale, his scent crawled up my nose, mixing with the air and seeping into my brain. Branding it and ensuring that I would never forget that masculine scent. Sandalwood and leather. Maybe it was because he was the first man to elicit a real reaction from me in ages. I'd dated over the years but never for very long or seriously. And now I was attracted to a man who was the head of a large—possibly shady—organization. Oh *and* he had people shooting at him.

"That's a whole lot of thinking going on for meditation time."

"Yeah," I sighed regretfully. "I told you it's been difficult for me lately but that doesn't mean that you can't get some benefits from it, Cross."

He unfolded his legs and leaned back on the grass. "I need it but I'm not sure it's working. All I can focus on is your perfume."

"Sorry. All the stress increased my pulse rate so I'm emitting all kinds of scents." *Did I seriously just say that?* "Sorry. Ignore the science lesson."

"I wasn't complaining."

I looked at him, his blue eyes were dark and full of heat. "Oh."

Luckily his phone rang and pulled us out of yet another intimate moment. "Shit. Yeah?" He held his phone up to his ear and frowned, standing to his feet with impressive efficiency for a man his size. "Fuck!" He looked at me apologetically, stuffing his phone in his jeans. "Sorry Moon, I've gotta go."

I stood and turned to him. "Go take care of your club, Cross. Be safe."

He nodded and smoothed his hands through his thick brown hair in a move I found impossibly sexy. "Thanks." He looked like he wanted to say more and I was very aware of how close we were. Too close. Then his hands were cupping my face and his mouth slammed down onto mine, tongue teasing me right from the start. His hands were rough and his mouth was soft yet firm. The kiss was fiery and hungry and when I opened for him, his tongue slid in on a groan.

It was the most explosive kiss I'd had in too many years to remember, so I squeezed my eyes tight and got momentarily lost in Cross. In his arms. His scent and that delicious mouth that tasted mildly of dark chocolate and cinnamon was irresistible. Intoxicating.

Addictive.

I couldn't get enough, moving closer to his body and it was hard. Everywhere. And suddenly I wanted more. More kisses.

More hugs.

More Cross.

He pulled back too soon and I moaned at the loss. "I gotta go. Really. But now I wish I didn't."

I nodded and walked him to the door because there was no way I would admit that I wanted him to stay.

Chapter Nine

Cross

Sleep wouldn't come for shit. Again. I wouldn't get anything accomplished by lying in bed and staring at the ceiling until my vision went blurry. Even Moon's breathing techniques hadn't helped, not that I would ever fucking admit to trying them.

Done with this restlessness, and with no plan in mind, I strapped on my bullet-proof vest, then some clothes, grabbed my keys and headed out the door. When I reached my bike I punched the air. Yes, I mouthed into the chill night. Suddenly sure of my next move, I jogged to the parking lot.

Since I still spent every night at the clubhouse, I had my choice of more than a dozen cars on the property. The dark green Toyota had keys in the ignition, so I turned over the engine and left the clubhouse in my rear view, heading toward a titty bar at the ass end of Mayhem. There was just one thing on my mind at the moment. Vigo. If I couldn't have any peace, neither would that fucker. He wasn't at the titty bar and after turning down a few offers for lap dances, I got out of there and headed to *Shandy's*.

He'd attacked a few of our probationary members there and though they weren't full Bastards, we would retaliate as if they were. *Shandy's* was a bust too and I felt my frustration growing by the second. All of this shit had started because of Vigo and it was hard as hell not to hold him personally responsible. What the fuck was he thinking?

He was a dumb son of a bitch which meant he wasn't thinking then and he probably wasn't now, and just like that I knew where he'd be.

The rundown, three-story apartment building where he'd met the woman with the bad dye job. I saw lights inside when I turned into the parking lot and shadows behind the curtains told me they were still awake. I didn't imagine that even as dumb as Vigo was, that he'd sleep away from the protection of his own home when so many people wanted him dead.

I waited.

And waited.

Pissed off and angry, I waited and let my anger fester and boil until it was full blown rage in search of a target. I wanted to pound something, preferably Vigo's face, until I was too tired to do anything but stop. It was all too much. The fucking city was screwing with us left, right and center, and I had no fucking clue why. Even after talking with Tanya again, I hadn't been able to figure it out. Yet.

"The inspector is off your ass. For now, because he didn't have a leg to stand on, but Cross these guys don't just randomly pick businesses to fuck with. They're like dogs, they go where they're told."

I'd replayed those words at least a thousand times since Tanya had called back and given me her expensive advice. The paper pushers had been sent by someone and not just some regular rich asshole, but someone with some actual juice to guarantee they didn't pay for their own crimes. I didn't have all the pieces yet, but I would. I'd taken the rest of Tanya's advice and had the guys go through every single business we had and make sure everything was up to code.

"Get proactive so the next time these fuckers come by, I can get them on harassment or something and earn that healthy retainer you pay me."

I'd just grunted and hung up, unable to see the humor in a never ending shit storm of stupid that had become my life lately. Just thinking about that shit again had even more anger pulsing through my veins.

Vigo chose that moment to leave the apartment, and I followed him as he took the backroads connecting Mayhem and Vegas that few tourists actually knew about. In many places the damn road got so narrow, I'd have sworn I was threading a needle.

A dark, cloudless night made it doubly hazardous. Tonight, though, the moon lit the way, the dented guardrails and handmade crosses testaments to all the people who'd met their end on this lonely stretch of road. Hollywood would have you believe the mobsters took people out here to kill them but the truth was it was almost always the desert that killed them. A ten-mile hike in the Vegas sun, or worse, the desert at night, would do in even the toughest mother fucker.

I thought about leaving Vigo to that fate, but he slammed on his breaks and jumped from that yellow target he was driving, which I filed away for another time.

"You stalkin' me, Cross?"

"Yep." No point in lying when his days were numbered anyway. I stepped out of the Toyota and stood beside it.

His eyes widened and though his chest puffed out, he didn't make any moves towards me. "You gonna do something about it?"

"Yep." The more he talked, the angrier I got. Thinking about Jana bleeding from the neck, Max's near homicidal rage until she woke up and Moon covered in Jana's blood. Yeah, this was the moment.

Vigo was twitchy, probably high. His skin was pale and even on this dark night I could see sweat dripping down his forehead.

"Yeah? What?"

His hand slid near his waistband and I knew what he was about, what he'd always been about.

"Reaching for that girly ass, pearl-handled pistol you love? Go ahead. Pull it."

I wanted him to, badly. But I hoped he didn't make me take him out too soon because I wanted to make him suffer. It was my duty as club president to see that he did.

With a sneer, Vigo brandished that gun and aimed it at me but I ducked behind the car door as two shots whizzed by the window. Hitting nothing. "I don't think so, asshole."

I heard the car door slam and the sound of his tires as he peeled away. I jumped up, hopping back into the car because there was no way Vigo was getting away. By the time he made it to the wide curve that would take us right to Las Vegas Boulevard, I'd caught up to him. It was hard to blend in when you drove a flashy car and when he hooked a right on East Harmon Avenue, I was right behind him, racing past the Hard Rock Casino.

"Keep running," I practically growled into my car and made a quick left onto Paradise Road.

Vigo thought he could outrun me and he probably had a few backup plans. But what he didn't know was that none of it fucking mattered. He was mine. Right after we passed the convention center, he turned right again down a quiet street. A dark and quiet street, but he kept going.

And going.

Finally, he must have got tired of running like a little bitch because he slammed on his brakes and got out, leaving his door wide open as he pounded his chest.

"You want me? Then come and get me motherfucker because I'm not running from you!"

"You should," I told him, deadly calm as I stepped out of the car, quickly gaining on him. "But it's your choice."

Vigo waited until I was just a few feet from him to throw his first punch, a jab that grazed my jaw and I stepped in and landed a jaw-shaking uppercut. "Son of a bitch! Bit my tongue."

I smirked and moved toward him, landing a jab square on his nose in a startling crack that sent blood flying everywhere. "Something you should have done before becoming a snitch. Was sucking that dead agent off required or just a bonus?"

He sneered and ran at me head first, intending to knock me on my ass but I wasn't having that. When he was close enough I lifted my knee and he went down instantly, writhing and crying in pain like the little bitch he was.

CREATIVELY CRUSHED

"You broke my nose!" He scrambled up, still holding his nose and throwing wild punches.

A few even landed, one to my right eye and another split my lip open, but it worked into my plan perfectly. While Vigo was feeling like a big shit, I found my moment and landed a hammer fist that sent him to the ground, me on top of him and I landed blow after blow on his face until my fists were coated in his blood.

Still I didn't stop. Couldn't stop.

Not until I could no longer see Jana bloody and unconscious, looking pale and small in her hospital bed. Max's face, scared and angry. Blaming me and rightfully so. By the time I stopped, Vigo's blood dripped from my hands and I could only stare in a wild, inexplicable fascination as droplets fell from me to him. I blinked to clear my mind and exhaled at the sight before me. I made it to my feet, breathing hard but grinning.

Vigo's face was unrecognizable, and his left eye was already swelling shut, but he coughed and groaned as he slowly got up. "You're a fuckin' dead man, Cross.

You and all of your bitches. Your whole goddamn club." He wiped his face with his hand, wheezing through his broken nose.

"You think so? I'd love to see you try." I walked away from Vigo while he continued to taunt me because I was stronger than him. Also because he'd stopped behind a bunch of shitty apartments where no one ever heard or saw a damn thing when the cops came to take statements. Vigo's laugh echoed in the still air as he got in his car and drove away.

He might have thought he was free and clear of me and he was probably already making plans for the rest of the Reckless Bastards, but Vigo didn't understand something very crucial. He was a dumb shit.

So goddamn stupid, he didn't notice when I pulled in behind his yellow and black eyesore. He didn't notice me behind the red Uber as he turned back onto Las Vegas Boulevard. I kept at least one car between us at all times, but it wasn't necessary, he was oblivious with his one eye swollen shut.

CREATIVELY CRUSHED

Four miles later ours were the only two cars on the same stretch of bad road, this time heading back to Mayhem. I let another mile pass before I stomped on the gas and passed Vigo on the left side, scaring the ever-loving fuck out of him when I honked and waved.

He tried to get ahead of me but, although that muscle car was sweet, it had nothing on a good old reliable Toyota. I was ahead of him and sliding back into the right lane in no time. Vigo tried to pass on the left but I moved at the same time he did, making a pass all but fucking impossible. "Try again, asshole."

He did. On the left side and the right side, before trying to pass on the left again. Then I made my move, slamming on the brakes so hard he had no choice but to swerve away or hit me. It was a calculated move, but I knew how Vigo would respond. The only way he could.

He slammed on his brakes and swerved to avoid a collision and flipped his own car in the ditch.

Two times. Three times. Four times before it finally stopped moving.

I stopped about a quarter mile up the road and walked back toward the already smoking car. "Help me! Somebody, help!"

That sound brought a smile to my face and I hated it, hated what this shit had turned me into. Vigo wouldn't be my first kill, nowhere near it. I'd killed for Uncle Sam and I'd killed for my brothers, but I'd never, not once, taken any joy from it.

Not like I was right now.

"Somebody call for help?"

"Fuck you! Get me out of here!"

"Your prayers have been answered Vigo. You wanted revenge for the death of your dumb fuck of a kid brother? Well you got it. Now you can go straight to hell and meet that shit stain."

"Please, Cross. Help me."

"Begging already, Vigo? I expected more." A spark caught in the engine and I took a few steps back, mentally calculating how much time before the fucker went boom.

CREATIVELY CRUSHED

"You know all those problems you're having with the city? I know the cause."

I froze. "Bullshit."

"Seriously." He was agitated, and his voice came out a shallow pant. "You think it's a coincidence that you fucked over that governor and now you have your own problems with the city? I. Thought. You. Were. Smarter."

His breathing was labored and even though I believed him, I had no forgiveness within me at the moment.

"And I thought you were smart enough to leave before it came to this. Turns out we were both wrong." I walked away, ignoring his cries for help, his agonizing screams and slid behind the wheel and drove away.

I'd made it about three miles up the road before a large plume of fire and smoke blossomed in my rearview mirror.

Good fucking riddance.

Chapter Ten

Moon

There was nothing like a long Pilates session to burn off some excess energy, especially when much of it was sexual and had to do with a man who was all kinds of wrong for me. Apparently that was my specialty and even though I was hot and sweaty and tired, I was not by any means, calm or relaxed.

I was still strung as tight as bow. Maybe a smoothie would help. It probably wouldn't, but that didn't stop me from pulling out all the fruit in my fridge in search of the perfect combination to soothe what ailed me. As soon as I figured out what that was. For now, a regular fruit smoothie would have to do the trick.

The sound of the doorbell startled me. It was early afternoon and Beau was in school. Everyone else I knew was at work or at home with their families. Given the events of last week, I made my way to the door slowly and looked out the window rather than the peephole. It was Cross. I pulled opened the door and gasped.

"What on earth happened to you?" I looked behind him to make sure he wasn't being chased and tugged him inside. Sweat matted his thick, brown hair to his skin and one eye had started to close around a bruiser of a black eye.

Despite the mess of his face, he tried for a smile. "You should see the other guy." His joke fell flat because I didn't find his behavior funny at all. I wasn't a pacifist by any means and I had a healthy respect for the fact that sometimes violence was necessary, but human life was fragile and I wouldn't pretend otherwise.

"Come on, tough guy." I pulled him into the kitchen and pushed him onto one of the cushioned chairs before I left him to gather my own first-aid kit. I had the usual bandages and ointments, but I'd added a few important items of my own.

CREATIVELY CRUSHED

"What happened?" I asked when I returned from the bathroom.

"Having a party?" he asked at the same time, his blue eyes eyeing my fruit selection with amusement.

"Making a smoothie. Now you, what happened?"

He shrugged. "Got into a fight and I didn't lose." He wasn't bragging and I appreciated that, but his matter of fact tone gave me chills.

But I couldn't focus on that. Right now I was in health care mode. "Are you hurt anywhere else?"

"That depends, are you gonna kiss it and make it better?" I knew he was joking for my benefit, so I shouldn't get too worried, but it was too late for that. I was beyond worried.

"Why did you come here, Cross? You don't want to answer any of my questions. You want me to stitch you up and send you on your way." It wasn't a question. I knew it as sure as I knew my own name. I set bandages and scissors on the table and started to mix a salve for the pain and bruising. "Comfrey is my favorite healing herb and I always keep it nearby for Beau's scrapes and bruises. This might sting a little but it's just the antiseptic."

"Holy fuck that stinks!" He leaned away from the bowl and held his nose but I wasn't deterred.

"You came to me, Cross. You either want my help or you don't." Arms crossed, I stood in front of him.

"I do."

"It doesn't smell the greatest but it works better than that drugstore crap." I put some witch hazel on the small cut on his forehead and applied my own antibiotic cream to his wounds. He was all patched up but everything about him was all wrong. I cupped his face and tilted it up until we were eye to eye. "What is going on with you, Cross? Your aura is a mess, but your eyes are…what's going on?"

"More shit than I need to bother you with," he spat out angrily, though I suspected that anger was directed at himself rather than me.

CREATIVELY CRUSHED

"Damn. I'm asking and it's my decision what burdens I carry, so don't be the hero right now. Just talk." I was the mother of a precocious eight-year-old boy, I could wait him out in my sleep.

I could feel Cross's tension across the room as I added blueberries, a banana, apple and plenty of other fruits and natural supplements to the blender. I added enough for two because whatever hell Cross was going through, he would need to be healthy for this fight. Filling up two tall glasses, I brought them to the table and set one in front of him. "Bon appétit."

Cross held the glass tentatively, eyeing the contents with skepticism before he put the glass to his mouth. "Damn that's good."

I shrugged. "It's just fruit."

"I couldn't sleep last night so I went out looking for the guy who shot up your shop. I found him too," he said with a sharp, bitter laugh. "We fought. End of story."

I nodded and listened carefully as he told me how he'd been stalking the man ever since that night. "I'm sorry you had to go through that, Cross."

"I didn't *have* to, Moon. I chose to, don't you see that?"

"I don't see it that way at all." Cross looked at me like he could see through me but I wasn't bothered because I knew for a guy like him, vulnerability was a new feeling. "You're the leader of a large family, Cross. And as the leader you have to do things you might not want in order to keep them safe."

He barked out another bitter laugh. "You don't believe that."

"I do. In fact, I used to be part of a large family so I know from experience."

"It's not the same," he said and I could see that he was determined to beat himself up over it.

"It is and when you're ready to accept that you did what had to be done, you'll feel a lot better."

CREATIVELY CRUSHED

"I shouldn't feel better," he growled and I could see just how torn up he was about this.

"I really am sorry you're going through this, Cross." I stood and went to him, wrapping my arms around him to give him the comfort he'd never ask for. It was meant to be platonic, just one human offering comfort to another but his arms tightened around me in a way that was more than platonic.

He buried his face in my cleavage with a groan and before I could voice my concerns about my post-workout sweat, his tongue slipped out and licked right between my breasts. "You smell good. So good," he said, the words gritty and drawn out.

My body responded instantly to the heavy need in his voice, the way he gripped me and held me close. His touch was hot and fiery, needy as he pulled me down onto his lap, not satisfied until we were so close not even a gasp of air could slip between us. Then his mouth was on mine and I was completely lost. Every sweep of his tongue, every time our lips touched was electric, combustible.

And I was on fire.

I never wanted the kiss to end, it was that good. So good I forgot about everything else but the taste of him, the feel of him. The way Cross made my body feel, like an exposed wire was being dragged along my skin. I couldn't get enough. The slow burn was nearly at a boil before his hands left my hair and traveled down my back, gripping my butt and pulling me closer.

The moment his hard cock came in contact with the space between my legs, I ached for him. "Cross." His name escaped on a throaty whisper as his hand slid down the back of my yoga pants and he squeezed my bare cheeks. He slid one finger deep inside me, at the perfect angle, drawing a long moan from me.

"Moon." His voice was deep and guttural, thick with his desire and need. He moved his finger gently, slowly, tapping on my sweet spot until I shuddered.

"Oh, God." I breathed out. It had been so long, too damn long since a man had touched me. And never like this.

Then, Cross pulled his fingers away and lifted me off his lap like I weighed nothing and put me on my feet, stripping me out of every stitch of clothing. The cool air hit my skin and my nipples pebbled. "Yes," he groaned when he saw them and pulled me closer, sucking one hard tip into his mouth until my head fell back and I accepted his delicious torture.

Cross teased and tortured me with his thumb and his mouth while he unzipped in one quick move and freed his long, hot prick from its restraints. He was so thick and so long, so magnificent. I licked my lips and he chuckled.

"Like what you see?"

"Maybe. You have something to show me I might like better?" I couldn't look away from the erotic sight he made, sitting at my kitchen table stroking his cock in invitation.

"Damn straight." He pulled me closer until I straddled his lap and sank slowly down onto him.

"You're big," I grunted as I willed my body to relax and take him deeper. "So big." I began to move, not looking away from him for one second, afraid I might miss something.

"You're good for my ego," he bit out and I just smiled.

Cross wanted to rush through it but I couldn't. Not now, not when he felt so good, so amazingly incredible that my body was ready to burst from pleasure. His blue gaze was so dark it almost turned black, but he seemed as unable as I was to look away while I slowly rocked against him, ratcheting up our pleasure by degrees. "Yes, yes!" I urged hungrily.

He gripped me tighter, thrusting up into me for all he was worth until my body trembled with my impending orgasm. Grabbing my hair and tugging it just hard enough to send another frisson of awareness through me, Cross licked up the column of my neck. "Oh fuck, Moon. I'm close."

"Me, too," I told him, forcing his gaze back to mine. My hips moved faster, eager to feel Cross even deeper. He filled me up perfectly, thrusting harder until he felt the small quivers start deep within me and begin to work their way out. "Really close."

His thumb settled right on my clit and that was it for me. I was falling apart all around him while Cross continued to pound into me until his own orgasm burst out of him. His face twisted in a beautiful kind of agony that called to me. Like the pleasure was too much to handle, so much that it caused him pain.

"Moon, fuck!" He grunted and jerked up into me a few more times before we collapsed onto the weight of the chair.

My body, slick with sweat, stuck to his and I was too sated to care. I couldn't remember the last time my body felt this good. "That was incredible."

"Maybe I should get beat up more often?"

"Definitely not," I told him and swiped a drop of sweat from his neck. "But maybe you wouldn't mind a shower?"

"With you?"

I shrugged against him. "You could just watch if you like." I slid off his lap and gathered my clothes before turning to walk up to the master bathroom. By the time I reached the third step, Cross was right behind me.

Then I was in his arms and we were headed to the shower for round number two, which was even hotter than round one. And round three was shaping up to be the best of all. Until the school called.

Beau had had another asthma attack.

Chapter Eleven

Cross

My dark office inside the clubhouse was exactly where I needed to be. It fit my mood perfectly, dark and sparse. The Reckless Bitches nagged my ass to let them fix it up a bit, but the small room suited me just as it was. Nothing wrong with the wood paneled walls and dark gray carpeting. The big oak desk was new, and the leather chair matched the one I had in the Merry Mayhem room, only a shade less fancy. I did a lot of Reckless Bastards business in here, but I didn't give a damn about how it looked.

The room did what it was meant to and I didn't need shit else, no matter what anyone else thought.

"Yeah?" I was a little gruff when the knock sounded on the door because I'd made it clear I didn't want to be disturbed.

Jag walked in, expression as stoic as always these days. Not that before Vivi, Jag was an effusive type of guy, but at least he used to flash a smile once in a while. Now it was like the guy didn't give a damn. About anything. "I got some of that info you requested." He walked in and sat down, all business.

"Anything good?"

Jag shrugged. "It's not what you want but after all the shit that just went down with Vivi, I can't be digging around in government systems the way I used to. But, what I did find is useful."

Staring at Jag looking lifeless and without energy, I could only feel like this was another area where I was failing my club. Part of me wanted to help him, the other part didn't give a shit. "What did you find?"

He pulled out a flash drive and he handed to me. I put it in the computer and nodded to Jag to come around and do his thing.

"Bill Pacheco, the city manager," he said over my shoulder, "has a twenty-one-year-old enrolled at

UNLV, but according to her professors she rarely attends class. It's because she's spending all day with her new boyfriend, Lu."

Lu? My eyebrows rose and Jag nodded. "Roadkill's treasurer?"

"Yep."

Shit. That was a connection I hadn't seen coming. "You think Pacheco would shit on us just to help some dude who's banging his kid?" We were getting into tinfoil hats conspiracy theory territory, but we had to consider it.

"No." He shook his head with more emphasis than he usually showed. "But I also don't think it's just a coincidence. Either she was put there by Pacheco to urge them on or Lu sought her out for some reason. Either way, it's pretty damn certain it has to do with us."

"Shit." He was right. Jag was the best damn analytical mind we had. He was quiet and good-natured, but we'd gotten a lot of good intel and planning from him. For all those reasons and more, I hated that he was hurting because it was, in a way, my fault. "Thanks, Jag."

"No problem," he answered quietly and stood, turning to leave.

"Jag, you good?"

He turned. "No, I'm not good man. My woman took a hit. For us. It fucking sucks, a lot. But I'll be fine. You don't need to worry about me or my loyalty. My head is in the game." This time he left without waiting for my response.

Left alone with my thoughts, which should have been centered on the club and all the threats coming our way, I could only think of one thing. Moon. My God she had been a surprise, a revelation really. She was sensual as hell, taking to fucking the way she did everything else, full of passion and heat. And her sexual appetite was bigger than I would've ever imagined, giving as good as she got. Moon wasn't shy about chasing after her pleasure.

CREATIVELY CRUSHED

And when she was in charge? Fuck, I'd gotten hard three times over the past couple days just thinking about how hot she was when she took charge. In control of her pleasure and mine was a role Moon had been born to play, but next time, and there sure as shit would be a next time, I was taking the lead. I'd show her a thing or two about how good it felt to succumb.

To pleasure.

To me.

Music started blaring in the main hub of the clubhouse, which meant the Bastards and Bitches had started to congregate there. It should've made me feel good, knowing that my brothers and the Bitches, felt safe enough to come here and get loose. No matter how dicey shit got.

But listening to the music and the increasingly louder sounds of people having a good time, drinking and smoking, and soon there would be fuckin' too, it all just made me feel old. Old as fuck, really. Like a lonely old man.

And that was exactly what I was, a lonely-assed grumpy old man with nothing to lose, leading a bunch of men who had everything to lose. What a fucking joke that felt like. My eyes closed as feminine laughter rang out and I tried to practice those breathing exercises Moon showed me. So far they hadn't worked for shit but I kept trying because Moon seemed so damn Zen all the time and I wanted some of that.

Hell, I needed it.

But every time I tried to inhale deeply through my nose all I caught was Moon's scent. It was floral and earthy and sexy. No it wasn't just sexy, there was a muskiness that called to mind sex. Specifically, sex with Moon because now I knew just how satisfying it could be.

And I wanted more.

So much more I could fucking taste it, but now was not the time. And honestly I wasn't sure there would ever be a time that climbing back into bed with Moon would be a good idea.

CREATIVELY CRUSHED

Which was too damn bad because now that I'd had one taste, it wasn't enough.

Chapter Twelve

Moon

It still felt strange being back inside the Rainbow Canvas, but with every day that passed it was easier to be back. Adding small touches, like changing up the art hanging on the walls and rearranging the supplies helped. It made the place feel new. Updated and upgraded rather than just put back together. I could stand inside and almost not see the remnants of that night.

Baby steps.

Customers were coming back, but Friday nights were still slower than usual. Maybe I should consider calling them off for a few weeks. Until people felt comfortable coming back here to have fun while they made art, staying open was just a waste of money.

The wooden chimes over the door tinkled and I looked up from the inventory sheets on the counter as a young girl walked in. Girl wasn't quite accurate though. She was young but twenty-something young in a tiny, dark blue denim skirt and a white tank top that showed more of her hot pink bra than it covered.

"Welcome to the Rainbow Canvas. If there's anything I can help you with, just let me know." It was my standard greeting and her little sneer told me she didn't appreciate the effort.

"Is it true you had a shooting in here?" Big blue eyes did their best to appear innocent and non-threatening but her moves were far too practiced.

"It is. Looks like gang violence is everywhere these days." The girl leaned in, hanging on to my every word. "The police have no idea who did it or why," I snorted for added effect. "Probably already forgot about it."

"That is so terrible," she replied but even that sounded forced and not even a little sincere.

"It was at the time, but life goes on." I knew when I was being pumped for information. I grew up in a house full of servants who felt nothing wrong with doing the job when my parents couldn't or wouldn't and they were more skilled than her. "So did you come for art classes or supplies, or to see where it all went down?"

I could tell that my tone had caught her by surprise but this was a business, not a tourist attraction.

"Is that okay?" She hunched her shoulders forward and shoved her hands into her pocket, in an effort to look more innocent, I guess.

"Sure. But if you're not a customer then I have other things to do." She seemed surprised but not offended when I went back to inventory slips that really didn't need to be dealt with today, but busy work made me feel like I was doing something. Anything.

She walked around the shop carefully. A little too carefully. I kept an eye on her, watching as she looked at everything then fingered several of the mid-grade brushes. But her gaze wasn't on the brushes or the palettes in front of her, but on the ceiling. More specifically, she was looking at the corners and light fixtures, for what, I had no clue but she was definitely searching for something.

She piqued my interest enough to make up my mind to do more than keep an eye on her. I pulled my phone from my skirt.

I have an interesting visitor. I sent Cross the quick, vague text message because he seemed so stressed lately that I knew he'd want to know this, even if I was reluctant to pass on any information.

Yeah, who?

I smiled. He was a man of few words. *Young girl, twenty-ish with dark hair and blonde highlights. Skimpy clothes and not a skilled interrogator.*

His response came within seconds. *Be right there.*

I should have known the man with so much on his mind wouldn't let this sit for long. *My house, not the shop.* I had to be careful on the off chance that someone was watching, because clearly they knew Jana, and possibly Rocky too, liked to hang out here.

CREATIVELY CRUSHED

"Thanks for letting me look around. You have a super cute shop!" With a wave and a blinding smile, she was gone.

My shoulders sank in relief the moment I saw her cross the street and walk out of my sight. That girl was some kind of trouble, I could just tell. A girl who tried that hard to be sexy usually ended up with men who had warped views of femininity and sexuality. It wasn't my problem but I committed her face to memory just in case it became my problem.

A tap at the back door interrupted my fifteen minutes of alone time. I knew it had to be Cross because Jana was the only other person who knew about the back entrance. A quick peek through the back door and I gave Cross the high sign to give me a few. I hurried to close up my shop, putting a sign in the front window telling customers I would "Be back later."

"Hey," Cross said the minute I stepped outside.

"Hey," I said back, unsure how to respond to him after our...*encounter*. And he stood there all expressionless like we hadn't had the most incredible sex of my life the last time we saw each other. Well, if he could do it then I could too. We walked the short distance to my house, as though nothing out of the ordinary had happened between us.

"So like I said, she had thick, dark hair with blonde highlights and she looked young, college age maybe. Her questions were pointed, about the shooting. And she kept looking around the place."

I could feel the tension coiling in his body. "Looking around at what?"

I shrugged, suddenly feeling uncomfortable. Where was the sexy but gruff man who'd rocked my world and why had this cold automaton showed up in his place? That was when I realized that the man next to me, *this* version of Cross, *this* was him. "I don't know. She touched the paintbrushes, palettes and mixers but her eyes were on the ceiling."

He fell silent and I waited until he gathered his thoughts. "Would you recognize her if you saw her again?"

CREATIVELY CRUSHED

"Of course, she was five feet in front of me the entire time."

"Is this her?" Cross shoved the phone in my face and showed me a photo of the woman who'd come into my shop, only she was missing her tacky blond highlights.

"Yeah, it sure is."

"Thanks." Apparently that really was it and I nodded my acceptance. I had no expectations of Cross other than basic human decency but it still hurt to be so soundly rejected.

"No problem," I replied because I would never in a million years make a fool out of myself over a man. Not ever again. I tried that once and I didn't like how it ended.

Before we even entered my house, he waved his phone at me in a sort of goodbye and turned back to his bike parked behind the shop.

***

I was just about to rinse the kale when the alarm on my phone sounded and I groaned. It was time to pick up Beau from school and get him to yet another appointment with Dr. Yang. His asthma attacks had increased in frequency lately, but not in intensity. Even though the episodes scared me numb, I had to believe he wouldn't have this horrible illness forever.

Luckily the appointment was uneventful, which I was learning as the mother of a child with a chronic illness was as good as it got. Other than an hour wait to get into the examining room, the appointment went as expected. No better but no worse.

On the way home I asked, "How are you feeling today?"

"I hate the nebulizer."

"Remember what we said about hate, honey." I didn't want him to grow up throwing around such loaded words when he didn't have to. This world was filled with too much negativity as it was.

CREATIVELY CRUSHED

Beau sighed heavily and pushed his glasses up on his nose. "Fine. I detest the nebulizer and I don't like the other treatments either. I just want to be like everyone else, Mom."

"What a boring place this world would be if we were all the same." It was a sentiment I wished my parents had told me instead of drilling conformity into me until I turned into the rebellious daughter they couldn't control. Until they gave me the message they didn't want me.

"You know what I mean, Mom."

"I do," I admitted on a weary sigh because I did know, and I understood more than he could understand at his tender age. "And I wish I could make it all go away, believe me I do. But for now all we can do is cope with the cards we have."

He frowned at me from the passenger seat, a tiny smile twitching on the right side of his mouth. "You said that wrong."

"Did I?" He gave an exaggerated nod but all I cared about was that his smile grew bigger and bigger. "What would you say about pizza for dinner?" Even though he didn't have a traditional diet, Beau was no different from any other kid who'd jump for joy at the mention of pizza.

"Okay." It was reluctant acceptance but I knew that wouldn't last long. "Key Largo's?"

"Where else?" I'd never ever set foot inside a tropical themed pizza parlor until moving to Nevada, but *Key Largo Pizza Haven* never did anything halfway. The goddesses must have been shining down on me because we found a spot inside the parking lot, not that it would make the wait any shorter but if Beau suffered another attack I'd have to carry him and for that, distance mattered.

The place smelled amazing, like it always did because for some reason coconut oil and pizza sauce worked together.

"Cross!" Beau darted between four tables, narrowly missing a pitcher of beer.

CREATIVELY CRUSHED

"Beau," I called, always worried when he ran when he should walk, anxious that exertion would bring on an attack. If only I had the secret to putting a level head on such young shoulders.

Then I spotted the reason for his excitement. Cross sitting by himself in a booth, a large pizza on the table in front of him. He looked good, even with the bruising. "Hey kiddo, how's it going?" I heard him say as I came up behind Beau.

"Okay," Beau said, pushing his glasses up again. "Did you get picked on too?" Beau pointed to his still healing busted lip and Cross grinned.

"People try to pick on me, but I don't let them, Beau." Cross turned to face Beau so they were eye to eye. "How are you, really? Your mom said you were having trouble breathing again."

Cross looked up at me with a look I couldn't decipher. "Hey, Moon." Was it pleasure at seeing me? Total disinterest? Why couldn't I read this man? Why wouldn't he let me?

"Hey, yourself, Cross."

I turned my attention to my son, and froze, waiting for Beau to clam up as he usually did whenever anyone mentioned his illness. But he surprised me, opening up easily. "I don't like the nebulizer."

I quickly changed the subject. "What do you want on your pizza, Beau? The usual?"

He didn't take his eyes off Cross, just giving me an enthusiastic nod, so I left Beau at the table while I went to place our order. I figured he would be fine for a few minutes since Cross appeared more amused by him than annoyed. Though I wondered about that flash of pain in his eyes I sometimes saw when he looked at my son.

It didn't take long to place the order but who knew how long the wait would be, so I took a moment and grabbed some vegetables from the salad bar. And I might have taken a small moment for me, away from Cross and his delicious scent before returning to the table, where Beau was talking about his favorite thing in the world. Sports.

CREATIVELY CRUSHED

"The Golden Knights are going to take the Stanley Cup this year," he said with an air of authority that had Cross covering his mouth.

"But what about those Sharks?" Cross asked.

Beau nodded and I knew exactly where this conversation was heading. Stats. "Yeah, but the Knights are—"

"—Eat some vegetables while we wait for our pizza." I slid the plate over and he carefully looked at the options before grabbing a baby carrot. "Sorry," I mouthed to Cross.

His mouth curled into an irresistible smile. "Don't be."

"I have a booster seat if you want one," the woman at the table beside us offered.

I smiled gratefully, Beau never used them even though he was a touch small for his age. "Thanks, but it's not necessary."

"What?" Cross looked at Beau who stood beside the empty chair warily. "How are you gonna stare your food in the face before you tear into it? You gotta show that pizza who's the boss."

Beau still looked wary but Cross picked up a slice of his meaty pizza and gave it a mean look before biting into it aggressively. "Aargh! See?"

And just like that Beau's hesitation vanished and he laughed hysterically. "Okay. Thank you, miss."

"Oh, aren't you sweet," the woman said, immediately stepping forward to place the booster on the seat beside Cross. "Enjoy your pizza young man."

He climbed up into the seat and waved at the retreating woman. "I can't wait to be this tall."

Cross chuckled. "Enjoy being a short stack while you can." He winked at Beau who tried a wink back as if he accepted the older guy's wisdom, and then picked up a carrot stick.

"Okay," he said simply.

And me? Well I had to send a wish out to the heavens above that it was just lust I felt heating up my insides and not something else.

Chapter Thirteen

Cross

"I'm leaving. Right now." It was the third time I made that particular promise with my lips hovering a breath away from Moon's. We didn't have much time left before Beau came home from school.

"You already said that," she shot back, her voice filled with heat and amusement. That pink tongue darted out and slid in a hypnotic motion from one corner to the next and I knew I'd say those words a fourth time. The tip slid along the seam of my mouth and I was lost to the electricity of the kiss. The heat and the hunger. She was like a magnet pulling me in and I was too needy to step back. To turn away.

I needed to be inside her. Now. "Tell me to leave," I growled because if she told me to, it was the only way I could walk away from her while my body trembled with need. A dark, hungry need that I couldn't deny.

"I will," she promised on a breathy pant. "But not yet." Then her mouth was on mine in that slow sensual way she had. Moon wasn't a rush through it kind of woman. No, she was the type to savor every touch and every taste. And right then she savored my mouth like it was one sweet morsel of chocolate. "Upstairs," she commanded in that low, husky voice of hers.

Moon only had to tell me once. My cock was hard—throbbing hard—and anxious to be inside her. I locked the front door before turning to follow her down the hall and up the stairs, smacking her ass once in a while just to let her know I was still back there. "Moon."

She stepped inside the bedroom and turned to face me, making my heart pound so loud I couldn't hear a damn thing. "You plan to stay over there, wearing all of that?"

"Fuck no." I stalked to her, my animalistic intent written all over my face as I took her mouth because I couldn't resist her sweet, pink lips, her hot, wet tongue and the way it yielded under my own. It was always like this, raw and greedy, and as I made love to her mouth and stripped her down, kissing her from her collarbone down to her breasts, the intensity never let up. I savored those beautiful breasts, pulling one nipple and then the other into my mouth until she arched into me with a moan.

"Cross, yes!" Long, nimble fingers tangled in my hair and pulled me closer. Like she fucking couldn't get enough.

Of *me*.

I listened to every gasp, every moan and every cry of pleasure as I kissed my way down her body, stopping at the curve of her hip to nibble. The soft flesh of her lower belly before I slid lower. And lower still until I was on my knees in front of her. Her legs trembled when I inhaled her spicy, erotic scent, and I let her fall to the bed, long legs hanging over the edge.

"Fuck," I grunted at the sight of her glistening pink pussy, clit throbbing just for me. My mouth watered and I bent low to satisfy my appetite, licking at her slick, pink lips and that bundle that called to me.

Lapping up her juices while she writhed beneath me, holding me close while trying to push me away.

"Cross," she said. Her tone was a warning. She was close and I was right there to push her over the edge. "Oh yes! Cross!"

The way she cried out my name hit me straight in the cock and I was ready to slide into her. But I didn't. Not yet. I wasn't done tasting her. Moon trembled when I licked down to her ass, sliding my tongue into that tight little rosette as she continued to writhe and pulsate.

"Cross!" When my finger slid into her pussy while I licked her ass like the sweet peach it was, she came apart and creamed all over me. My name on her lips. "Incredible," she sighed as the last tremor shook her body. Then a laugh escaped, nervous and wild. Sexy as fuck.

"Not sure a laugh was what I was going for." I stood and licked her from my fingers before I took off all my clothes.

CREATIVELY CRUSHED

"It was uncontrollable. Sometimes you feel so good that a laugh is the only way to express it." The way Moon looked at me, like I was her last meal on earth, had my cock standing up and taking notice. Leaking with his excitement to be so close to where he wanted most to be.

"Come here," she crooned.

"Gladly." After climbing on the bed and hovering over Moon, I wrapped an arm around her waist and lifted one long leg over my hip, leaving her exposed to me. "Ready?"

She nodded and arched into me. "More than ready. Please, Cross."

She cried out as soon as I thrust deep, body moving to catch the rhythm. She rolled her hips with me, allowing me to sink deeper and deeper into her delicious wet pussy.

"So fucking wet," I groaned. She was responsive as hell, taking little more than a nibble on her ear to drench her panties. "Moon."

Her head pounded into the pillow, again and again, and she moved one of my hands to her tit, urging me to squeeze, to knead while she kept up a symphony of erotic noises that made it harder and harder to think about her pleasure.

Her cunt pulsed around me and I lost it, gripping one hip so hard I knew she'd bruise but I couldn't think straight while her pussy clenched tight and trembled around me. Her orgasm was right there, building while I threw more kindling on the fire by arching her back so I could fall deeper inside her.

"Oh fuck, Moon!" I pinched her nipple and she fell apart, shattering all around me, pumping and pulsing while I kept fucking her until that tight cunt pulled my own orgasm from me. "Ah, fu-uuck!"

She continued to vibrate, to shake with the aftershocks of her orgasm. Her pussy pulsed hard, still squeezing me until I pulled free and every drop of cum covered her round, pale ass cheeks.

"Wow!"

CREATIVELY CRUSHED

Her breaths came in hard and fast. Another blast escaped but it was me this time.

"Told you," she said on another laugh.

I could listen to Moon laugh all night, especially if that's the sound she made between orgasms.

"You're insatiable."

She laughed again but this time it was more amused. "You do something to me, Cross. It's like you just know all the buttons to make me off the chart explosive."

I would never get tired of her blunt honesty, especially when it came to praising my skills in the sack. "I hate to argue with you Moon but I think you might have had something to do with that."

She nodded, now focused on catching her breath as she turned on her side and faced me. "So hot."

My lips curled into a grin. "Thanks."

Her expression turned serious and I got nervous. Moon saw too damn much and right then I didn't have enough brain capacity to hide from her. "How are you doing, Cross?"

The only reason I didn't get the fuck up and walk out was because Moon seemed to genuinely give a damn. Her eyes were sincere and I knew she wouldn't press it so I felt okay giving her a bullshit answer. "I'm okay but not good. Hell, I'm not even better. But I'm working on it." My sleepless nights and racing thoughts were all that fueled me to keep going for my guys. My family.

"All you can do is work on it." Her words were simple and easy but the kiss she placed on my chest was something else altogether. "And ask for help when you need it."

There it was. The advice I really didn't want to fucking hear. "I don't ask them for help, Moon, they come to me for help. That's my role as President."

"That's crap," she sighed, calling me on my bullshit without using the profanities that laced my words and thoughts. But never Moon's. "You know what, Cross? You remind me of my father, always so stubborn and so sure he was always right and knew everything. He made all the decisions and the rest of us could either fall in line or fall away. Never asking any questions or input from the rest of us." She sighed and laid those eerie green eyes on me. "He thought he was being a strong leader but you know what the rest of us thought? That he didn't have the faith or confidence that any of us had anything valuable to contribute."

There was so much information contained in those few short sentences that I wanted to dissect and ask follow up questions, but Moon was too good for my clumsy conversational skills. "Sounds like you have a very interesting family."

"Had," she corrected with a hint of sadness in her eyes. "They're alive but we are what you might called *estranged*." With a shake of her head she used her hand to prop her head up to look at me. "My point is that you are stronger together. Combined, you guys have the skills to accomplish just about anything. You are the leader Cross, without a doubt. But that doesn't make you the expert in all things. Let your men do their part to help figure out whatever's causing you stress."

It was a valid point. One I would take into consideration. Later. When Moon's hand wasn't grazing down my thigh and wrapping around my cock, stirring him to life. Her tongue licked up the side of my neck and a groan escaped. "Is this some new motivation technique, because I think it's working."

She laughed and pulled back, her gaze glued to mine as she kissed her way down my body, stopping to explore and tease some parts more than others. "Is it?"

I nodded but my eyes were closed tight and my head thrown back as her lips wrapped around my cock, disappearing into the wet heat of her mouth. Moon handled my cock like she was the one getting pleasure from sucking me off, moaning as she took me deeper and deeper. Her tongue swirled around the sensitive head until I shivered and bucked into her mouth. She didn't choke but opened right up and I thought I might die right there on the spot. "Fucking heaven."

CREATIVELY CRUSHED

My hands went to her hair and she didn't even flinch when my grip tightened and I began to thrust down her throat. Instead, she fucking moaned and took me as deep as she could.

She fucking *moaned*.

My phone rang and vibrated somewhere on the floor. "Fuck."

She laughed around my cock but, woman that she was, Moon didn't stop. Instead she took me so deep I could feel her tongue swipe against my balls.

Little temptress was feeling playful. "Yeah," I grunted into the phone.

"You need to get to the clubhouse ASAP," Lasso said without his usual over the top greeting. "We have visitors."

The rest of his words were nothing more than white noise as my head began to spin and my heart pumped into overdrive. "Shit. Okay." The call was over and my cock was still buried in Moon's mouth which meant I had to say the three words I really didn't want right now. "I gotta go."

She looked up with a smile. "Two minutes?"

"Ambitious."

She accepted the challenge in my voice and arched a brow. "Confident," she shot back before those sinful lips enveloped my cock again, sucking me deep and hard. Ninety seconds later I filled her with my come which she took like a pro before turning onto her back with a moan.

Silence passed in the room as I slowly got dressed, trying to focus on Lasso's words about the visitors. "Sorry."

"Don't be. I had fun but life has a way of intervening, doesn't it?" She didn't want an answer which was good because I didn't have one. "Everything okay?"

Damn her and her sincere worry. "Yeah. Two detectives showed up at the clubhouse. No big deal."

CREATIVELY CRUSHED

She groaned and rolled her eyes, making me wonder what a hippie soccer mom artist had against the police. "Good luck."

I smiled and dropped one final kiss on that sweet mouth. She didn't know just how bad I needed some good fucking luck.

***

I hopped on my bike and hauled ass back to the clubhouse. There was only one goddamn reason two detectives would show up and ask for me by name. Vigo fucking Rizzoli. Even in death that motherfucker was causing me problems but I knew the routine. They would press and I would give them nothing because I didn't talk to cops if I didn't need to.

I took one minute to get myself calm before dismounting my bike. The detectives stood about ten feet in front of the clubhouse entrance and I walked slowly up to them because there was no way in hell they would get inside without a warrant.

"Detectives, I hear you're looking for me." I knew these guys. One was a regular cop and the other was a fucking asshole.

"Yeah." That was the older cop with the hair that was more gray than brown these days. "We have some questions." He took charge of the interview. "You're familiar with Vigo Rizzoli?"

"I am, but I assume he left town, considering."

"Considering what?" The little one, Dodds, puffed his chest up and took a step forward. I stared at the pissant and waited for him to make his move or back the fuck up. "Well?"

"Is that a question, because I'm not sure I understand it." The little one opened his mouth to speak but I turned back to the other detective, Haynes. "I assume you do know that he owns a car that looks a lot like the one that shot my friend? In the neck?"

CREATIVELY CRUSHED

"And I guess you're seeking retaliation?" The little one was determined to edge his way in to this conversation and I was just as determined to keep him out.

Haynes nodded. "That's why we're looking for him."

"Yeah, me too. If you see that asshole tell him he better hope his club gets to him before I do."

The little one laughed but Haynes barked at him. "Dodds!"

"What?"

"Shut up." He turned to me, a question in his eyes. "Why is Roadkill after one of their own?" Haynes listened and took notes as I told him.

"He's a snitch and he was working with the feds. You know as well as I do, his days are numbered either way."

Again the older detective nodded, his pen hovering over the pad. "Where were you three nights ago?"

"Here, like I always am. Why?"

"Because we asked you, that's why." Dodds wore a sneer as he leaned forward, his eyes growing wide with fear when I leaned in too. He was a pussy, just like I thought.

Haynes sighed like he had the weight of the world on his shoulders and I imagined as a homicide detective in this city, it was. "We found Vigo's body last night, badly burned. Looks like he lost control of his car, flipped it and got stuck inside before the damn thing exploded."

"Shit," I replied on a whistle. "Couldn't have happened to a nicer guy." I couldn't help but smile knowing that Vigo was rotting in hell where he belonged.

"And you had nothing to do with it?" Dodds asked with his trademark sneer. When it was clear I wouldn't answer he tried another way. "I heard you're making life difficult for Stuart Roundtree."

CREATIVELY CRUSHED

That shit just pissed me off. "Really? Did you also hear that he came here and tried to shut me down for not supplying him with information he had no fucking jurisdiction to see? Or do you bend over for all city officials, corrupt or not?"

I smirked at the way his eyes went wide and his nostrils flared in anger. He stepped forward, too damn close for my liking but I allowed it.

"Say that again," he sneered like the reptile he was.

"Put down your gun and badge, rookie, and I'll give you the ass whooping you desperately want." I puffed my chest out until he had to step back to look up at me.

"That's it asshole, you're under arrest."

"Yeah?" I looked to Haynes. "I'm pressing charges. Police harassment," I shouted and pulled out my phone and hit speed dial.

"Tanya, I need you to file a harassment complaint against Detective Dodds. No first name, but I got his badge number." I rattled it off to my lawyer but kept my eyes on that shifty fucker.

"Put the fucking phone down! You're under arrest!" Dodds put his hand on me and I shoved him, which only pissed him off even more.

"Don't fucking touch me!"

Haynes stepped between us, face red and pissed off. "Dodds, get in the fucking car! Right now!" The commotion forced a few of the guys inside the clubhouse to step out, making sure I didn't need their help. Haynes held his hand up to stop them. "Not now, guys. Stay where you are so I can settle this without the bracelets."

I held a hand up to let them know it was all right to stand down, holding my phone up to see that, like the incredible lawyer she was, Tanya was still on the call.

"Fuck that," Dodds spat at his partner. "That asshole—"

CREATIVELY CRUSHED

"No, Dodds, not now. Get in the fucking car before you make things worse for yourself." Haynes stood between us until the asshole turned and walked his stubby ass back to the unmarked cop car.

Haynes turned to me with a weary smile. "Pressing charges against him won't make things better."

I knew that but I didn't care. "You might be right but I don't like him and I don't trust him. With all the weird shit going on lately I need my complaint to be official." If there was some hinky shit going on with the government, that Dodds guy would be involved.

He nodded again and took the statement. "You'll have to come back to the station to sign it and make it official."

"I will," I assured him and I'd make sure Tanya came with me.

"And watch yourself, Mr. Wylie. There is some weird shit going on and I don't know what, but I can feel it in the air."

A sardonic laugh escaped me. "You too, huh?"

With a tired nod, Haynes turned and walked away, giving me the perfect opportunity to flip off Dodds, who watched angrily before returning the gesture.

What a fucking asshole that guy was. It almost made me *hope* he was dirty, because then I might get the chance to end that fucker.

Chapter Fourteen

Moon

Business at the shop still hadn't returned to normal so I closed up early, feeling out of sorts and not wanting to face an empty house. Times like this reminded me how important it was to have a life for myself outside of work and Beau. I'd been fooling myself these past few years, preaching the benefits of a work/life balance, while hiding in my own stressful world of being a single mother and small business owner. I failed miserably at that balance, so today I decided to work on it by making an unscheduled visit to Jana.

I felt nervous standing on her doorstep and waiting for her to answer. What if she was busy? What if she didn't want to be bothered and felt obligated to entertain me? I'd just talked myself out of my foolishness when the door opened to reveal a very pregnant Jana. Smiling. "Moon, hey."

I froze at her tone. "Did I come at a bad time? I just wanted to check on you, see how things were going."

"No, you're right on time," she said in a tone I couldn't quite pinpoint, but I followed her through the house and out to the backyard where Rocky and Teddy sat on blankets while the babies played in the sun.

"Oh! I didn't mean to crash your party, Jana." Mortified, which was something I hadn't felt since leaving the suffocating arms of my family, I stopped before the cement turned to grass. "I'll catch up with you another time."

"You damn well won't. Get your butt over there and sit down with the others who just *wanted to check in*," she said with a smile that took the sting off her words. "If I was a suspicious sort, I'd think you all planned this."

CREATIVELY CRUSHED

"Certainly not. I closed up early and thought it was the perfect time to catch up with a friend."

"If that's the case then you know you aren't intruding and you're just being weird."

I laughed. "I'm always weird."

"I know. Come on."

I joined the women on the blankets laid out to accommodate curious babies and toddlers. Charlie, Jana's first born, climbed into my lap and began playing with my colorful necklaces hanging low enough for his curious hands. I laughed and tickled him playfully. "Hey Charlie, good to see you too."

He giggled and his attention turned to the string of turquoise around my neck. First he played and tugged on them but inevitably they found their way inside his mouth.

"Mommy," he said around the beads and held them up for Jana's inspection.

"Sorry about that," Jana said with a smile and a sympathetic expression.

"Don't worry about it, I made it myself with nontoxic paints and topcoats. It's just a bit wet and I'm used to it. When Beau was a baby he was fascinated by my colorful outfits and jewelry, so I began to wear more of it just for him. Except for earrings. I stopped wearing them because he kept pulling them out of my ears."

"You did?" Teddy seemed impressed by my handmade jewelry, which surprised me. This was the same beautiful woman who always dressed like she just stepped off the runway. Today she wore casual denim capri pants and a soft green tunic and looked like she just came from a photo shoot.

If Teddy hadn't been so down to earth I'm sure I would have felt intimidated. As it was, I explained how I shared my creativity with Beau.

"I've always loved art and when Beau was young it was a good activity to do together. You should see some of the pieces he's made for me over the years."

I laughed to myself as I remembered. They were crooked or cracked and over-painted but I loved them and wore them. But I thought, enough about me. I turned to my hostess. "How are you feeling Jana?"

"Yeah, Jana," both Rocky and Teddy said at the same time, drawing a laugh from me.

"I'm fine," she sighed like a woman sick to death of answering that particular question. "The doctors are keeping a close eye on me until the wound is completely healed, in case the unexpected occurs. But I'm fine."

"Good," Rocky said with a hint of fatigue in her voice. "Because I have something else to talk about. Lasso. He's so stressed out but he won't say what's going on other than 'some shit,' which doesn't exactly say anything to me about *what* specifically is going on."

She let out a long sigh when she finished and flashed a sheepish smile. "Sorry."

"I'm just glad it's not just me." Teddy leaned back on her hands, head tilted towards the sky. "Golden Boy has definitely been stressed and we both know it's not the shop or money issues. If it was, the handsome bastard would tell me all about it." She rolled her eyes for good measure but there was an affectionate lilt to her voice. "Something is going on. Definitely."

I didn't know what to say because I shouldn't know anything about this problem, but I did. Only it wasn't my problem to talk about. I knew one thing for certain, though, Cross was an immensely private guy and would not appreciate the women worrying over a problem he'd barely shared with his guys. So I stayed silent. "Isn't that the nature of...things?"

"That doesn't mean we have to like it," Rocky shot back with a defensive tone.

"Right. Well I should get going." I'd only been there a little over an hour but I'd rather be alone than sit through this tension. "It was good to see all of you." I waved and stood, bending to help Jana when she tried to get up quickly.

"Don't go on my account," Rocky said, her expression half apologetic.

CREATIVELY CRUSHED

"I'm not. I have to pick up Beau." I left the turquoise necklace with Charlie, who was too mesmerized to do little more than wave goodbye. I turned and walked away, practicing my deep breathing exercises as I made my way to Jana's sunny yellow front door.

"You don't have to go, you know."

Jana had caught up with me. "I know I don't have to but I should."

"You're one of us."

I wasn't but I appreciated her saying so. "No, I'm not Jana and that's fine. You and I are friends, so I hope you know you can talk to me about anything, but I do know that Club business isn't any of *my* business and honestly I'm not sure I should hear it."

"Why not?" The question was genuine, evidenced by the confusion written on Jana's face but just as quickly that confusion turned to suspicion and I realized my mistake.

And shrugged it off. "Just seems like the less I know about it, the better." That much was true. All the information I'd gotten about the Reckless Bastards was happenstance, nothing I needed to know about because I didn't have a personal connection to them.

"But you knew enough to call Cross about the trampy girl in your store, right?"

Shock must have shown on my face because Jana grinned and leaned against the back of the sofa. "Max isn't quite as tight lipped as the others because he knows I won't tell or go off half-cocked angry at someone in the Club. And because he doesn't want me to worry."

"I knew the big guy was a sweetheart."

"Yeah, he's great," she said dismissively. "You called Cross?"

"No, I texted him. And I did that because her questions were clumsy and she admitted she just came by to see where the shooting happened. It was nothing but it occurred to me he might want to know." And again, based on Jana's expression of know-it-all happiness, I knew I'd said too much.

"But you knew his number to text him?"

I nodded. "He feels responsible about the shooting and has been checking in, that's all Jana." She was blissfully in love and therefore saw it everywhere she looked.

"Maybe. Maybe not. But you could be good for each other. You could soften his edges, and he could be a man strong enough for you to lean on."

I barked out a laugh. "I lean on myself, Jana." And a professional if it came to that, but I didn't let it. Not often, anyway.

"You can't do that forever," she said softly and raised her hands. "I'm not saying anything more on the subject, I swear. Except that Cross could use a woman like you in his corner."

"I doubt that." Cross was an island. A man fully self-contained who didn't need or want anyone or anything but his club. The Reckless Bastards were all that mattered to him, leaving any woman who fell for him on her own. He didn't want me, other than for a few nights, or anyone else for that matter. "You see love everywhere and I love that about you."

"And you are an excellent subject changer," Jana said, accepting my hug before shoving me out the door. "Talk soon!"

I waved as I made my way back to my car while hoping it wasn't too soon because I had a feeling Jana wasn't ready to give up on her matchmaking.

***

"Mom, where is your mom and daddy?"

Beau's question had literally and figuratively knocked me right on my butt. In fairness, I was twisted up under a cubbyhole trying to retrieve a paintbrush when he asked his question, sending me tipping over onto the gleaming wood floors. "It's where *are* they honey, and they are where they live. In New York." This wasn't the first time he'd ever asked about my parents or his father but somehow, he still caught me by surprise. "Why do you ask?"

He shrugged. "Just wondering. Sylvester is spending the weekend with his grandparents."

I knew the time would come eventually when Beau wanted to know more about his family, but I always assumed it would be questions about his father. Those questions didn't have many answers but these did. "You know your mom is a bit weird right?"

He giggled and nodded his head, blue eyes lit with amusement. "Yeah but a good weird."

"Thanks, but your grandma and grandpa didn't think so. They wanted me to be one way and I just didn't fit. Eventually we all just thought it would be better if we lived separately." That was the redacted, PG version of what happened, but in a nutshell, it was the truth.

"So I won't ever get to see them?"

And there was the rub. I couldn't keep Beau from them if he wanted to meet them, but I was terrified that my father would reject my little boy the same way he'd rejected me. "I wouldn't say never, but I haven't spoken to them since before you were born." Not for lack of trying on my part.

"Okay, Mom. But you'll try?"

"For you, I will do more than try, Beau." It was a promise I'd made while Beau was still in the womb, and I had no plans to break it.

"Thank you."

"You're welcome. Got it!" I held up the paintbrush triumphantly and Beau clapped.

His eyes went wide, though, and he looked past me through the newly replaced front window and my blood ran cold. The sounds of someone trying to open the locked door drew my attention and I turned around.

"Go to the back, Beau."

"But, Mom I'm not—"

CREATIVELY CRUSHED

"Now, Beau. We'll finish up later." He nodded and hurried to the back, giving me a moment to collect myself before I went to the door.

"Can I help you?" It wasn't very professional of me to ask through the unopened door. But I didn't know this man and through the glass I saw he was a white guy with white-blond cornrows and a vest that looked similar to Cross's. Only not.

"Yeah, you can open the door lady." He pulled on the door again, impatient now.

"I will. Tomorrow when the shop opens."

His icy eyes seared through me, somehow hot and angry. "I need to get in now."

"Why?"

"Because I do lady, now open the goddamn door!" He began to kick the glass with his boot, soft at first but it grew harder and harder just to show me he could.

"One second," I told him calmly and walked over the counter where the cash register sat, unused for days, and grabbed the handgun I kept there. I'd never had occasion to use it because, despite its name, Mayhem was a pretty quiet place to live. If you didn't count the odd drive-by shooting. I returned with the gun in my hand but hidden behind my long, bright skirt.

"What's your name?"

"Craig," he shouted, finally no longer kicking my door.

"Craig what?"

He glared but I glared back, knowing I had the upper hand. I hadn't been to the gun range in more than a year but this was a stand your ground state and I was only two feet from the door.

"Well?"

"Craig Jefferson."

"And what do you want, Craig Jefferson?"

"I want you to open the fucking door before I kick it in."

CREATIVELY CRUSHED

My first thought was *this is perfect,* but then I remembered, Beau was in the back. Alone. If something happened to me this dirtbag would probably hurt my baby just because he could. I turned the lock and stepped back quickly, which was smart because the jerk was inside my shop in seconds.

 "What do you want?" I asked, this time more forcefully.

He took two steps forward and I lifted the gun, forcing him to put his hands in the air with a greasy smile. "Hey, lady, I just want to talk."

"You threatened me and my shop. Start talking or I'll be telling the police a different story when they get here." And because I'd always wanted to, I pulled back the slide and put a bullet in the chamber. "Start talking Craig Jefferson."

"I'm looking for a friend."

I scoffed. "I'm sure we don't travel in the same circles."

"Maybe not but I need to find him."

"I already told you, I don't know your friend."

"Think. Hard." His expression turned hard, menacing.

I slid my finger to the trigger and curled it around it. Wordlessly. The threat was clear. "I gave you my answer. Take it and leave."

"Damn!" Craig licked his lips and gave my body a long, thorough perusal. "Now I see why Cross is keeping you all to himself."

I laughed. "If Cross is guilty of anything, it's being too stubborn to realize that dirtbags like you don't even register on my radar." I laughed again because I figured being bat-shit crazy on top of armed was even scarier. Right?

"You don't scare easy for a dirty hippie. That's okay, I can make you real scared."

"It's *really* scared, but that's not the point. I get it, you're a bad scary guy. The thing is, I don't care. I could shoot you right now and not even your mother would care. But I'd care, so please don't make me shoot you."

CREATIVELY CRUSHED

"You've got a kid back there." His spine straightened and I aimed the gun higher in response, making him smile.

"Which is the only thing making me think that killing you right now is a good option." And that was the honest truth.

The wooden chimes sounded on the door, drawing my attention and Craig's so I pulled my finger from the trigger and lowered the gun. Half way because the thing about being from a rich east coast family was…hunting. Detective Haynes walked in with his irritating partner. And Cross. "Did I have an appointment scheduled?"

"Is that thing legal?" Dodds barked out.

"Of course it is, but seeing as I didn't invite you into my shop, which is closed by the way, maybe you want to tell me why you're here?"

"We have news." Detective Haynes stepped forward so he was face to face with Craig. "But first I need to know what I just walked in on."

"Easy. Mr. Craig Jefferson here kicked my door and then he threatened me, so I grabbed my *legal* handgun and let him in where he started questioning me about a friend of his, who I'm sure I don't know."

"This friend have a name?" Dodds again, so eager to play with the grownups.

I looked to Craig and then all eyes were on him. "Vigo."

"Thought so," Cross said from the back, eyeing Haynes with a hard expression before he walked over to me.

Detective Haynes sucked in a deep breath and blew it out, his tired eyes on me. "We believe Vigo was the one who shot up your shop."

"Vigo who?" I asked. "I'm sure I'd remember someone with a name that unique."

"Vigo Rizzoli," Dodds shouted. "Where were you last week from late Thursday night to early Friday morning?"

CREATIVELY CRUSHED

So something had happened to this guy, Vigo. I could answer their questions but Dodds was a jerk and I had a feeling the man with his hand resting on my back might know what happened to the guy who'd nearly killed Jana. "Sounds like I should consult my attorney before answering that question. If that's all gentleman, the shop is closed today for a reason."

Haynes sighed again and glared at his partner. "We do have questions, Ms. Vanderbilt."

"I see that, but my attorney will insist on being present for the kind of questions you have, Detective." I almost felt bad for Haynes but just like he had a job to do, I had a responsibility to protect myself and my son.

"Here's my card. Have your attorney call to set up a time. We need to talk."

"Or you could just tell us now and we'll be gone," Dodds offered with a grimace that was probably meant to be a smile.

"Maybe next time you'll be a little nicer to the citizens you get paid to serve. Have a nice day and please, don't come back here harassing me, not even if you need art supplies." My shoulders sank in relief when the three men left and Cross locked the door behind them.

"Exciting day?"

A tired laugh burst out of me. "A bit dramatic for my taste. What brings you by?"

He smirked and grabbed one of my curls, twirling it around his finger. "I came to tell you about Vigo and ran into the cops outside. Were you really gonna shoot White Boy Craig?"

Another laugh burst out of me at the absurdity of that name. I guess a woman named Moon had no room to talk, but still. "I didn't want to, but I would have if I needed to."

"I'll just bet you would. Where's—?"

"Mom! Is everything all right?"

CREATIVELY CRUSHED

I gasped and went to Beau, nearly falling backwards because I forgot Cross was attached to me by the curl. He released me and I sprang forward, wrapping my arms around my little boy. "Everything is fine, Beau. Just fine."

"Mommmm, too tight."

"Sorry." I stepped back and that gave him the time he needed to peek around me to Cross.

"Mr. Cross!" He darted around me and came to a near skidding stop, right in front of Cross. And then he wrapped his arms around him. "Hi."

"Hey, kid. How's it going?"

"Okay. How's your scars?" He reached up to touch Cross's lip and when he grinned in return, I felt things I shouldn't have.

"Better. How's your breathing?"

"Better. You want to have dinner with us?" Finally realizing he wasn't the adult in this family, Beau turned to me with wide, pleading eyes. "Right Mom?"

"Sure. Cross is welcome to join us for dinner but only if he's available. Remember?"

"Right. Are you available for dinner?" Beau asked in an almost grown-up way.

Cross couldn't stifle the laughter this time. "Let me check my schedule and I'll let you know. Think I can have a couple minutes to talk with your mom?"

Beau nodded and walked away, almost certainly to the book he had tucked away in the back.

"You're good with him." He was better than good, and Beau ate up his attention, starved for it since he'd never had much male influence beyond a teacher here and there.

"He's a cool kid."

Cross was the best. Maybe too good.

"So this Vigo character is dead?"

"Yep. Car accident." I arched my brows when he flashed one of those heart-stopping grins at me and I felt my knees buckle. "That's the truth."

CREATIVELY CRUSHED

"Works for me. I assume you have an alibi?"

"Don't need one because I didn't do anything. I just wanted you to know he won't be bothering you again."

Cross really was sweet even though I knew he'd balk at the word.

"You don't have to come for dinner if you don't want to. I'll explain to Beau."

"Are you taking back my invite?" His mouth spread into a grin that I didn't just want to kiss, I wanted to devour it.

But that wasn't why he was here. "It's not my invitation to rescind, Cross. I'm just saying that you don't have to feel obligated."

"I don't. I'm hungry and glad that I'm getting a home cooked meal." He patted that flat and hard stomach that I knew was covered equal parts in muscle and body art.

"You'll have to set the table, though."

"I can handle it, Moon."

Not once since I legally changed my name had it sounded so good on another person's lips. Especially those lips. "Then let's go do it. Dinner. I mean. Let's go *eat* dinner."

"I'm game, either way, baby." His smile looked like it came straight from the devil himself.

And I may—or may not—have melted on my way to get Beau.

Chapter Fifteen

Cross

What the fuck was I thinking making a statement like that? I wasn't thinking. Couldn't possibly be thinking to have said some shit like that, because Moon was a mom and I had to remember that. There was a reason I hadn't messed around with single moms because they deserved better than a man like me. Especially these days. I let Lauren down and I wouldn't put myself in that position again.

"You okay, big guy?" Moon looked at me with a worried grin that I found far too appealing.

"Yeah, just wondering when I last had to set a table." Lauren used to set the table because she loved to make shit beautiful but that was years ago and the Reckless Bastards weren't the table setting type. Unless a woman was involved.

"Well I figured I could use you since I'm cooking. Beau gets to see a big strapping man setting the table."

I wiggled my eyebrows at her. "You think I'm big and strapping?"

When Moon laughed she did it with her whole body, bent over with her shoulders shaking and her hair falling everywhere. "I think we both know that I do. How have you been sleeping?"

Nothing got by this woman and I needed to remember that. "A few hours here and there."

"And the breathing exercises?"

My lips quirked up. "You know I've been working on it but, you see, I have this problem. Whenever I breathe in real deep the only thing I can smell is you."

She shivered. Even with most of the kitchen between us, I saw it. "As flattering as that is, if you don't get enough sleep you won't be able to do much about it, will you?"

"Right to the point, huh?"

CREATIVELY CRUSHED

"Mom says there's no time to waste!" Beau went into the kitchen and pulled the silverware from a drawer and came up to me. "I'll go behind you."

I put a napkin down and then a plate and the kid came up behind me and set a knife and fork on each napkin. It was a little two-person assembly line and after one quick spin around the table, we were done. "Thanks," I said.

"Welcome. Want to see my room?" The kid definitely didn't waste time and he wasn't shy about asking for what he wanted.

"As long as your mom doesn't need any more help." I didn't want to be just another mouth for her to feed.

"I'm good. You guys go have fun and Beau?"

"Yes, Mom." He sounded like an annoyed teenager.

"Let Cross get a few words in too, okay?"

"Okay, Mom!" He rolled his eyes and signaled me to follow him. "You can talk first. Did you always ride a motorcycle? Is that your only motorcycle? Do you drive it in the cold, too?"

This kid was something else for eight years old. Talkative and kind and smart. As hard as it was to sit with him that day at the hospital, just a few weeks ago, it was now easy. Relaxing, even. "Not until I was twenty but I always wanted one. I do have a car and yes, I ride my bike in the cold."

"Can I ride it?" He pushed open his door and I stared into the ultimate boy's room. His bed showed his love of science and space, with a big swath of stars on it. But his walls were an eight-year-old's fascination with sports, the walls plastered with baseball, football and hockey posters.

"I think we both know that's up to your mom." And I had a feeling she wouldn't want her son on the back of motorcycle. And I didn't blame her. "So what do you like to play with?"

Beau showed off his shelf of Legos, then talked and talked, which explained why Moon had warned the kid to let me get a few words in. He never ran out of breath. But I liked listening to him talk about his love of hockey—even though his asthma didn't allow him to play sports—his fascination with going to space and finding new planets. His love of all things with wheels.

"Do you like sci-fi? Mom's letting me watch Star Trek on Netflix."

"Which one?" He shrugged and looked up at me with those big, all-seeing eyes.

"Do you have a family, Mr. Cross?"

"No Beau, I don't. I had a wife but she got sick and died." I hated even thinking about it and I couldn't believe I just told that shit to a kid. This was why I wasn't fit to be around kids.

His eyes went dark and I couldn't read them, but then he said, "That sucks," and it was like he could read my heart.

Damn. This kid had the soul of an old man. "Thanks, man. I appreciate it. Now tell me about that big stacks of books over there."

He smiled at me and I knew it was the right question. Besides, being around Beau and Moon, especially now with all this shit swirling around inside of me and this fucking town, it made me feel a little less broken and scarred. A bit more normal.

For now, it was enough.

Chapter Sixteen

Moon

Days after Cross had joined us for dinner, I couldn't stop thinking about what I'd overheard outside Beau's room. He was a widower and from the sound of things, Cross still suffered from the loss. It explained the sadness I often saw in his eyes. Every time I thought about it, my heart broke for him all over again. And to top it all off, the way he talked to Beau about it, so matter of fact, was perfect.

So perfect that Beau hadn't stopped talking about Cross since he left our house that night, which made it impossible to stop thinking about the man. And I really, really needed to. A few sessions of unbelievably amazing sex was no reason to start obsessing about a man, especially one with so much on his plate already.

I shook thoughts of Cross out of my mind as I pulled up in front of Beau's school. Today was the last day of school which meant three months of me and my favorite guy hanging out and having fun. But first we had an important appointment with a new specialist.

Even though Beau was smarter than the average kid, I knew the time would come when he'd find hanging out with his mom boring and uncool. So I knew I had to savor every moment he still thought I was the best thing since chocolate pudding. My heart swelled and a smile spread across my face as I caught sight of his black hair flopping against his forehead.

"Hey buddy, how was your day?"

Beau climbed into the front seat and I immediately heard the wheezing and slight effort to breathe. He eased his backpack over the back seat and I knew he was having a bad day. No energy to bounce into the car, fling his backpack around, give me a high five and start his nonstop chatter.

He slumped back and fastened his seatbelt without a reminder. He wasn't having a full-blown attack, just a routine struggle with asthma. I wanted to scream out to the heavens and pound the steering wheel but if he could deal with it without complaining, I could too.

"It was good, Mom." He said the right words, but his tone told me otherwise.

"Are you upset about the specialist visit? If you are, don't worry. This is just informational."

Dr. Yang had recommended that we see a new doctor who used stem cells to treat certain asthma cases. I didn't know a lot about stem cell treatments other than they were showing promise for patients with plenty of ailments, so I was cautiously hopeful.

"No Mom, it's not that." Well, it was something and the way his bottom lip poked out told me it was a serious something. I waited. Beau was male, albeit a young one, which meant he wouldn't share his feelings until he was good and ready.

Waiting was easy once I merged into traffic and listened to NPR playing low inside the car. After fifteen minutes he pulled out a book and called my bluff. That was what happened when you had a kid too smart for basic parenting techniques. I let out a heavy sigh as I turned off the radio.

"You have to be the only kid on the planet who isn't happy on the last day of school."

He sighed and shoved his book into the side pocket of the door. "They want to put me in the fifth grade next year instead of fourth."

It wasn't all that shocking since his teacher and principal had been hinting at it all year, but I didn't like that they'd gone behind my back to talk to my kid about it. "You don't want to do that?"

"Noooo…how will I make friends with those older kids?" He looked up at me like I had all the answers.

I wish I did. "Easily. You're funny and great, how can they not want to be your friend?" His blue eyes showed me that he didn't appreciate that answer and my heart ached in my chest. "Science camp starts in a few weeks, chat up a few of the older kids if you can. Maybe you'll have a few friends when the new year starts."

CREATIVELY CRUSHED

"But Mom, it's fifth grade! After that I'll be in sixth and then comes junior high and I'm not ready!" His cheeks were bright pink, and his eyes had turned pale in his anguish.

"If you're not ready then you don't have to do it, Beau. But I think you should think about it for a while before we do anything. Okay?"

He nodded but I knew he wasn't finished. I could feel his gaze burning through the side of my face. "Can we forget the appointment today? Nothing will ever work and now I have to think about the fifth grade," he said as though it were on par with trying to pursue world peace. And to him, I was sure it was just as important.

"Tell you what, you think about the fifth grade and I'll worry about the specialist." It was the best I could offer because I would never stop trying to help my little boy. Whether he was eight or eighty, I'd always do whatever I could to give him the best, longest life possible.

The drive to Dr. Mankowski's office would go quickly as soon as we moved away from the city traffic, so I relaxed behind the wheel and listened to Beau talk about all the experiments he wanted to try when camp started. Last year he'd gone to math camp, but he hadn't enjoyed it quite as much. "I like science more than numbers," he said, remembering his disappointment last year.

"You don't think math is useful?" I asked.

He rolled his eyes. "I guess it's useful, but with science, you can see how it works in the real world."

I laughed. "And you think math doesn't?"

He shook his head. "No, Mom, you don't understand."

"Well, I could argue the basics like paying bills and buying groceries or making a cake but let's go a little more difficult and talk about critical thinking skills. Buildings."

"But buildings also use science," he argued correctly.

CREATIVELY CRUSHED

"I think that means they're both very useful in everyday life."

Beau groaned. "I guess so."

By the time we arrived to see the specialist, Beau had forgotten all about becoming a fifth grader next year. I just hoped the doctor had some good news for us.

***

Visits to doctors and specialists had always left me feeling exhausted and even though I knew I brought it on myself, I couldn't stop it. The incessant worrying and waiting for the other shoe to drop. The clenched fists and teeth, and of course the racing heart. But today Dr. Mankowski had given me something I'd been faking for a long time.

Hope.

He hadn't made any promises but his research was promising. And it gave Beau a chance to get off the nebulizer.

"Don't be scared, Mom," he said on a yawn. Poor Beau was even more beat than I was after plenty of breathing tests as well as a physical exam and a quick blood test to see if there were any other health concerns he needed to know about before they started determining his eligibility for the stem cell treatment.

I sighed and ruffled his hair. "You're a sweet boy, Beau, but you know I will always worry about you. Always." We were almost home and I needed peace. Maybe yoga. Maybe a magic brownie once Beau was down for the night.

Maybe. It was the story of my life. *Maybe, maybe, maybe.*

A quick look in the passenger seat showed his eyes had slid shut and his chest moved up and down evenly. No wheezing to be heard as I turned into the driveway and that fact alone had my whole body sinking back into the driver's seat. Hearing him breathe slow and normal was a load off.

For now.

His attacks came at any time and they could be light and quick, no big deal. But most of the time they were more serious, exhausting for both of us and often ended up with us in the hospital emergency room. I had hoped we'd both end up in our respective beds today.

But as I looked through the windshield my gaze landed on Cross, looking better than my black bean lasagna and I already knew he was twice as delicious. What I didn't know, as I stepped from the car and rounded the trunk to get my sleeping son, was why he'd shown up on my doorstep.

"Hey." The word came out soft, quiet and maybe just a little breathless. Maybe.

"Hey." His smile was as bright as I'd ever seen it, even though the shadows were still there.

"Everything all right?"

He blew out a breath and took Beau from my arms while I searched for the keys I'd dropped back in my handbag.

"Yes and no."

My chuckle came out low and amused while I pushed the door open, stepping aside so he could take Beau in first. I followed, doing my best to keep my gaze off his perfectly rounded backside which was encased in deep blue denim that showed off long, sculpted legs to perfection. He was a treat to look at and just like any treat, it was all right to indulge once in a while.

Cross laid my little boy in his bed like Beau was as precious to him as he was to me and I knew that would be a hard image to forget, especially as Beau grew older and asked more often about his father. But I was getting ahead of myself.

"What else?" Cross asked.

I smirked at how uncomfortable he looked, all big and tall and masculine in a room meant for a small boy. "You want to get him ready for bed?"

CREATIVELY CRUSHED

Cross's face dissolved in a look of horror, and I had to bite my lip to stop the laughter threatening to wake up Beau and make for a cranky little boy.

"I'm kidding. You can grab a beer if you want or take some time to find some other creative ways to get out of talking about what's bothering you."

I swear his face held a distinct pink tint as he brushed past me, his leathery masculine scent invading my nose for long moments as flashes of the physical pleasures I'd found with him played in my mind.

"You're a regular comedienne aren't ya?"

I shrugged. "Nope. Just a teller of unfortunate truths." I left Cross with that thought as I quickly worked off Beau's shoes, socks and jeans. He hated sleeping in his t-shirt and undies because he thought it was too childish but he'd never had the unfortunate task of trying to undress his sleeping form. After a quick kiss goodnight, I pulled the door closed, leaving a small gap because I was an overprotective parent to my core.

"You're good at that stuff." Cross's voice startled me in the dim hall. "Sorry," he said, looking more amused than sorry.

"It's okay." My smile was a little wobbly as my heartrate returned to normal. "And thanks," I said, sidestepping him as I made my way down the staircase. Distance was key when Cross was fresh from the shower, smelling like a man with slightly damp, chocolate hair. "Every day it feels like it's all one second from disaster so don't let this cool shell fool you. I'm told it's normal but that doesn't make me feel any better."

"I couldn't tell. You look like you're killing the whole parenting thing."

A laugh exploded out of me and I smacked a hand over my mouth, frozen in case Beau woke up. "Thank you, Cross. That's nice to hear. Drink?"

"Sure." His lips quirked up like he knew I was trying to change the subject. "I never thought you'd be uncomfortable with compliments. You seem so confident."

CREATIVELY CRUSHED

"I am, but any parent who is confident is probably doing it wrong."

I'd seen all types of parents and had been raised by two supremely confident parents who, if they weren't rich, would have been prime candidates for neglect convictions. I grabbed a bottle of wine from the fridge along with some cheese and crackers. I didn't tell him the hors d'oeuvres were my own recipes; I figured he was dealing with enough hippie dippy food as it was. And accepting it pretty well. I didn't want to push my luck.

"Grab those glasses, would you and follow me."

Cross followed me into the backyard, setting the glasses on top of the colorful three-legged table I'd painted with Beau a few years ago. "Cool table."

"Family art project." The two Adirondack chairs were as colorful as the table. "Pick a color."

He grinned. "You know I have to take the one with the cape on the back," he said with a laugh as he lowered himself onto the chair. "I always wanted to be a superhero."

"I'm sure you'd look fantastic in tights." He cut me a glare that made me laugh again and finally I felt the last of the tension seep from my body. "Very fantastic."

He popped the cork and frowned. "What the hell is this? Moonshine?"

"No, because this isn't the 1920's, and its blueberry wine. I picked it up at the Farmer's Market." He still looked skeptical but I filled both glasses to the halfway point because it was clear Cross had something on his mind. "Drink."

Despite his tough guy persona, Cross was openminded, sniffing the aroma before taking a small sip. Then a bigger one. And a bigger one still. "Damn that's good. Better than I expected."

"It's made by a local artisan. She also does a fantastic blueberry kush wine." The surprise that flashed on his face was damn near comical. "It's delicious too and has a low alcohol content."

CREATIVELY CRUSHED

"Why didn't I know about this?" he grumbled.

"Probably because from what I understand, your dispensaries aren't licensed to sell booze. Anyway she only sells them at the market, so if you're interested you need to get up early on the weekends."

Quiet settled between us, both lost in our own thoughts. My head was tilted toward the sunset, as I enjoyed the last splashes of light before it began its final descent while Cross stared into his glass. It was nice but I knew he didn't come to spend time with me. "Ready to talk?"

He sighed, a universal male sign for he absolutely did *not* want to talk. I wasn't surprised. Disappointed maybe, but Cross didn't owe me anything so no, not surprised. "There's not much to say, Moon."

"I hear you, but your aura is vibrating red and black, which means you have a lot on your mind and whatever it is, there's danger associated with it and possibly death." I didn't want to tell him what else, but I had to. "And you don't know where all the threats are coming from."

His blue eyes were obsidian with nothing but the fading sunlight surrounding us, but I could see the emotion written all over his handsome face right now. Shock. "How in the hell could you possibly know that?"

I was used to that response when I offered an analysis because people always vacillated between shock and anger, sometimes defensiveness and accusations. "I just told you, red and black surround you like Deadpool."

He wanted to say more, to question if I really saw it or had another source for my information. Thankfully, he didn't. He poured more wine and took his time finishing the glass before he spoke. "You're right and you know almost as much as I do about it. Roadkill is one of our problems even with Vigo now worm food, but I can't say for sure where the other threat is coming from. But fuck, it feels like something is coming. Something big."

"Are you ready for it, whatever it is?"

He huffed out a purely masculine laugh. "Fuck no."

CREATIVELY CRUSHED

I stood and reached for the blanket I used as a cushion on my chair, fanning it out on the ground. "Come on, sit. Take off your vest, your shoes and any weapons you have."

"Weapons?" Thick brown brows arched in a question.

"Yeah, aren't people trying to kill you?" Arms crossed, I dared him to argue.

"And I suppose you don't have any weapons around?"

I heard the challenge in his voice and raised my chin in defiance. "I'm used to being underestimated," I told him. "When I was younger, I hated it. It always bothered me. And then I grew up. I accepted it for the advantage it gave me." The look on his face when I pulled the butterfly knife was priceless. "See? That advantage."

His smile curved up, highlighting his soft lips and the sparkle in his eye. "You never fail to surprise me, Moon."

"I'll take that as a compliment," I told him and sat on the blanket with my legs folded in front of me. "Sit here." I patted the space right across from me and when he sat, our knees brushed. His scent and his heat swirled around me with the impact of a tornado, making it hard to focus.

"Okay. Now what?"

"Now we breathe." He groaned but I held a serene smile. "Not deep breathing necessarily, just calm breaths. Listen to my voice and breathe like this." His gaze tore through me as if he could see more than I was allowing, which was somewhat unsettling. "None of that."

"None of what?"

I pointed at his face. "None of that heat and desire. We're being calm. Relaxing."

"I'm getting very relaxed." His gaze turned predatory, intense with a raw hunger I'd yet to see on his usually stony expression.

"Pay attention," I admonished, and he only smiled again.

"You have my undivided attention Moon."

Why did my whole body light up like a Christmas tree when his voice pitched low like that? Probably because I knew he could more than match the promise in his gaze. His intoxicating voice. I shook it off because I had to, because Cross needed me to. Sex was amazing most of the time and so far with him it had been better than ever, but it wouldn't fix this.

"Focus," I told him and closed my eyes, continuing the deep breathing exercises while letting the sound of his breathing slow my own.

"This isn't working." Cross sounded frustrated but I kept my eyes closed and reached for his hands.

"Give it time." It didn't always work but with a little effort, I knew it could help him clear his mind and focus on the big picture.

"I have a better idea." His voice was a deep growl, forcing my eyes open. Reluctantly.

They opened just in time to see his handsome face twisted with desire and heading my way until his big body pressed against mine, slowly leaning me back onto the ground. "This isn't the right position." But it was one I enjoyed as his denim-covered cock settled against the wet panties that separated us.

"But it is a pretty damn good position. Right?" For emphasis his hips moved against mine, sending a fiery trail coursing through my veins and a starburst behind my eyes.

"Yep. Very good. Very."

Cross chuckled at my words and once again I was struck at how much that one move transformed his face from the hardened president of a motorcycle club to a boyishly handsome man with eyes that lit up beautifully. "You're too damn distracting, Moon."

I loved the way he said my name, low and gritty and hungry. Like he really meant his words, not like he was playing games. "I think that's my line."

CREATIVELY CRUSHED

Cross was done talking, I could tell because the air around us changed. Sharpened. It was electrified as his expression turned serious and his hand began a slow journey up under my skirt, big and hot, leaving a trail of heat until he reached my core. "Fuck. You're so hot."

I laughed. "So are you. Scorching."

He licked his lips, gaze fixed on mine until he closed his eyes and laid claim to my mouth in a kiss so hot, so fiery and so raw with obvious need that I couldn't resist it if I tried. I could do nothing but arch into him, open myself to allow the invasion to be complete. And then—sweet goddess above—his fingers hooked inside my panties and slipped inside where I was wet and hungry for him. "Fuck. So fucking wet, Moon."

"You do have that effect," I told him, breathless with need and arching up into him because my body wanted everything he was offering. One finger teased me at first, slowly pumping into me but mostly teasing me until I moaned. "Tease."

He laughed and pressed his lips to mine again, this time plunging two fingers deep, pumping into me while his thumb teased over my swollen clit. I swallowed his groan while my hips rolled against his hand, silently begging for more.

I didn't know how long we stayed like that, making out and heavy petting like kids decades younger than us, but I relished it. I reveled in the way Cross made me feel, wanted and passionate and young. It was an intoxicating feeling that I couldn't get enough of, not yet anyway. Not when he tore his lips from my mouth and slowly began a wickedly sensual form of torture all around my neck while his hands brought me close to the edge and backed off.

Once.

Twice.

And just when I was about to get angry at his teasing, Cross pushed me over the edge, pulling a low erotic moan from me. "Cross!" My chest heaved, and my overheated skin didn't seem to recognize the chill in the air because the sun had set long ago.

CREATIVELY CRUSHED

"I love to hear you shout my name when you come apart."

"Yeah? Well if you have a condom we can test that theory." I wasn't uptight about sex but given my living situation, I wasn't careless either. Even though I couldn't resist Cross, I knew I had to be careful.

"I don't but that's okay, it was just for you. I got exactly what I needed."

I didn't know what *needed* meant but there was no way in hell I'd let him leave unfulfilled after those intense words.

Chapter Seventeen

Cross

The one fucking night I was actually *asleep*, a call woke me in the middle of the damn night. "What?" I didn't bother checking the screen because calls this time of night were never good news.

"Yo, Cross, we're at the Stetson—"

"I'm fucking sleeping, Stitch," I barked into the phone, now fully awake.

"Yeah, I figured but some guys and I were here, just to make our presence felt, ya know, and the police showed up. Trying to arrest Katrina."

Shit. Katrina ran Stetson, our more upscale brothel where guys paid a fuck ton of money to fuck girls slightly prettier and in more expensive lingerie than Bungalow Three. "Fuck. I'm on my way. Tell Kat don't say shit to them." I ended the call and swung my legs off the bed, rubbing my eyes. I went to the bathroom to splash cold water on my face.

I had one call to make as I pushed out of the back entrance of the clubhouse and hopped on my bike.

"Tanya. Cops are at Stetson and I need you to scare the fuck out of them and keep Katrina from getting arrested."

"Oh goody, I was starting to think you boys had forgotten about me. Meet you there." She disconnected the call without further details but I knew better than to question Tanya. She was a badass. A total fucking ballbuster and I was happy as hell to have her on our team.

When I walked inside the brothel and saw Katrina in handcuffs with tears pooling in her big brown eyes, I saw red. Pure white-hot fucking rage surged through me at the sight of Dickhead Dodds standing there with a uni as green as a fucking meadow. I wanted to bash the fucker's head in but I waited. No blood would be shed until Tanya showed up.

CREATIVELY CRUSHED

Dodds sneered, so fucking happy with himself. "Which of our girls are you enjoying the company of this evening, Dodds?" I stopped less than a foot from the little sniveling fucking piece of shit. "Don't know if they told you but there are no dudes in here."

"Real funny Cross. Won't be so funny when I take your whores in for questioning."

I tossed my head back and laughed. "And where exactly will you take them, Mayhem? Oh right, this isn't Mayhem and therefore not your fucking jurisdiction." I looked around. Where the fuck was Tanya? "I guess you boys want to give us some more of your operating money."

"You fucking bikers think you run this shit. Well, you don't."

"Actually we run this business. This legitimate fucking business that helps pay the salary of bloated pigs like you." I wanted him to give me a reason. This fucker would be worth the jail time.

Just then I heard the sound of high heels clacking against the wooden floor, but the sound came from the rear of the building.

"Ah, there you are." Tanya breezed in, her normally bone straight hair was curled into a bun at her neck but that was the only concession she'd made to the late hour, looking crisp in a red dress and matching jacket. "So what's going on here, Officer?"

The uniformed officer slid a wary gaze to Dodds, unsure what to say or do, which said everything I needed to know about who'd started this shit.

Luckily my high priced mouthpiece stepped in before I knocked his teeth out. "Tsk, tsk Detective. You were very naughty, being a bad boy and attempting to operate outside your jurisdiction. What a pity since we filed the formal complaint yesterday."

Tanya tapped her chin, deep in fake thought while her black nails, tipped with diamonds, were on full display.

CREATIVELY CRUSHED

"Sounds like retaliation. Maybe even malicious prosecution."

That's why we always paid Tanya. Always. She relished taking down assholes like Dodds. Just like I expected, Dodds stepped forward but the move wasn't well thought out because he now had to look up at Tanya.

"Your madame here failed to get a minor's identification," he insisted.

Tanya smiled that predatory smile of a woman before she rips a man's nuts off and shoved them down his throat.

"Is that the story you want to go with? Both of you?" she asked again and looked to the uniform who was now visibly sweating.

"That's what happened," Dodds insisted with more force than certainty.

Tanya turned to Katrina with a sympathetic smile. "It's up to you Kat. Do you want to spend a night downtown and make a shit load of taxpayer money for wrongful arrest or do you want to sleep in your big comfy bed tonight?"

Katrina blinked and looked to me for guidance. "It's up to you, sweetheart," I said.

She nodded and swiped her tears. "I'd prefer to sleep in my own bed," she answered quietly.

"Excellent choice, Katrina. Why choose one when you can have both?"

She winked and turned back to the cops.

"This is the alleged underage customer you're speaking of, I assume?" She handed him a large print out of the Nevada license with a triumphant smile. "See, everyone's ID gets scanned before they walk through the front doors. Including one Melvin Duane Dodds. Such an unfortunate name," she said and held an identical photo with his license up for inspection.

"Give me that!" He took a step forward and to her credit, Tanya didn't budge as she let the photo fall to the floor. "I can arrest you for attempting to blackmail an officer."

CREATIVELY CRUSHED

"You can try, *Melvin,* but we both know you'd lose and I'd own your crappy little bungalow and fifteen year old car. Those handcuffs on Kat right there constitute kidnapping since you have no legal authority in this town. In fact, I'll get my paralegals to start on the lawsuit right now."

Dodds stood there, nostrils flaring and face turning a hilarious shade of pink as he flooded with embarrassment. But the man wasn't as dumb as he looked and knew when to cut his losses. "This isn't over."

"Oh, not by a long shot, Melvin. We're just getting started," Tanya promised. "And don't forget to take your handcuffs or I'll be forced, as an officer of the court, to speak to your superior officer about this." How she managed to sound sweet as apple pie while issuing a threat I'd never know, but it was damned impressive.

"I have every right to investigate a crime," he grumbled as he yanked the cuffs from Katrina's wrists.

"We both know that's not true. So either you're here as a paying customer or a crooked cop."

"Bitch," he grumbled and walked away to the sound of Tanya's raucous laughter.

"God that was fun!" She turned to Stitch with a hungry glare. "Can you get me the footage from the moment the cops hit the property until about," she looked down at her watch, "five seconds ago."

"Sure thing, sweetness."

She tried to look perturbed by his words but even Tanya wasn't that good an actress. "You boys," she said instead before turning to me. "Never a dull moment with the Reckless Bastards, eh?"

I raked a hand through my hair, angry and frustrated. Ready to fucking blow my lid. "Thanks Tanya, but this shit has got to stop. What can we do?"

She put a sympathetic hand on my shoulder and sighed. "We'll figure it out. I'm working on it. I know you have your own sources, so just keep me in the loop and I'll fix it. That's what you pay me to do."

CREATIVELY CRUSHED

Tanya was right. And, she was one of the most capable women I'd ever met. "Fine."

"Great. I'll talk to you in a day or so after I make sure Dodds' boss knows what the little shit has been up to. Have a good evening everyone!" She rushed out damn near as quickly as she entered.

Now that the drama had passed, a few of the girls and their guests wandered back to the common area and I smiled at Katrina. "I guess your emergency protocol works."

She looked up, pale and shaken, with a watery smile. "Yeah. Sorry about all this."

"You didn't do anything wrong, Katrina. Not one goddamn thing. This is on us, but I promise you I'm gonna fix it. Don't worry."

"I'm not, but thanks anyway, Cross."

Thanks? She was thanking me for nearly getting her locked up. "One of the guys will make sure you get home okay."

"Thank you. You're a good man, Cross."

I snorted at that but offered up a weak smile before I left, barely able to keep my eyes open. I was headed home, but as I passed a familiar intersection, the desire to turn right and then left in front of the little house with vibrant shutters and tons of plants all around all but killed me. I wanted to go see Moon so bad. But, she didn't need this shit in her life, not as a single mom and definitely not with a sick fucking kid.

So once again I denied myself the pleasure of her kisses and aimed my bike toward home.

***

"Hey man, you got a minute?" Jag stood in the doorway of my office with a blank expression on his face and I hated like hell that I could no longer read him. He was quieter than normal and sullen all the goddamn time. Not that I blamed him. Hell, some might argue that I'd been nursing a broken heart for too damn long, but that didn't mean I had to like it.

"Yeah, come on in. What's up?"

"I've been doing some digging," he said as he walked in and closed the door behind him, as clear a sign as any that he had something serious to discuss. "I came across some campaign contributions that I'm pretty sure are going to Pacheco filtered through a bunch of shell corporations. I just can't be sure yet."

"But?" I'd known Jag long enough to know when he had more to say.

"But I'm pretty sure it's coming from Roadkill. Why else wouldn't they have handled Vigo immediately? No other MC would've let him live as long as they did."

Shit. Jag was right. "That has to be the missing piece. I've been racking my brain trying to figure out why the fuck they hadn't killed him, yet, *and* why he'd stuck around Mayhem for so long. Now it's all starting to make sense. In a fucked up kind of way."

"Yeah. I'll keep digging for connections between Pacheco and Roadkill and I'll let you know what I come up with." Jag was eager to leave my office and though I'd never admit that shit to anyone, it stung. I knew better than to take it personally, hell I'd shut damn near everyone out after Lauren and my baby died. But, Vivi wasn't dead. She'd be back. Lauren wouldn't.

"Thanks, Jag. When, or *if* this shit ever ends maybe you should take some time off and head east."

He froze. "Not until she's done with her time." Jag looked at me like I was singlehandedly responsible for Vivi having to work for the government to pay off her crimes. And *ours*.

"I did what I had to, Jag."

His black brows rose in surprise but that was the only indication of what was going on in his mind. "Never said you didn't."

"Jag," I began, frustration and weariness in my voice.

"No, Cross. You're my leader and my brother, but I don't wanna hear this shit. You're still grieving over your wife so don't give me shit about Vivi, yeah?"

CREATIVELY CRUSHED

He was right. I nodded. "Okay. Thanks for the info. I appreciate it."

"Just doing my job, man." With another blank expression and another nod, Jag left me alone again with my thoughts, which seemed to switch between all the trouble the club had been having to the bohemian sexy mama who'd completely captivated me.

What could possibly be more fucking complicated?

Another knock sounded, and I bit back a groan. I'd never get through the actual work I had to do with these constant fucking interruptions. *Probably means I should go to my real home.* "Yeah?"

The door opened and Gunnar strode in with the same pissed off scowl he'd worn since he'd come back to Mayhem. He stalked in silently except for the loud thudding of his heavy feet, took a seat in front of me and scowled harder. "We need to talk."

"I'm listening." Gunnar was an ornery son of a bitch on the best of days but now with his estranged mom dead and his baby sister in his care, he was just a dick. My brother, but still a dick.

"There's too much fucking shit going on around here Cross. Too goddamn much."

"Yeah, tell me about it Gunnar, because I have no fucking clue," I spat out. They didn't know half of what I knew because if they did, my guys would burn this fucking town to the ground to go after these assholes. But we needed a more stealth approach, so I kept some of the bullshit from them.

Gunnar's shoulders fell. "I know you know, Cross. You're the best fucking Prez we've ever had, and I don't doubt that shit. Not ever, so don't fucking think it. But I have to think about Maisie and man, this shit hasn't died down since I got back." His eyes seared through me like a laser.

Shit, he was serious. If I was having any thoughts about whether or not my leadership had failed the Reckless Bastards, Gunnar had just confirmed them. "You sayin' you want out?"

CREATIVELY CRUSHED

He sighed, and a ball of acid bloomed in my gut. "No, man. I don't want out. I need a break. Out of fucking Vegas. At least for now. I can barely take care of Maisie and I can't risk her getting hurt because of this shit with Roadkill and whoever the fuck else is fucking with us."

That was some fucking relief. "You know I can't just let you go. We have to vote on it." I told him.

"I know. And I don't want to leave the club. I just wanna get out of Mayhem for a while. You know how fucking hard it is to raise a kid?"

No, I never got the chance.

"I can imagine. But not until this current bout of bullshit is over. I need you here, Gun."

A wide grin spread across his face and I knew I needed to get used to not having Gunnar around. He was as good as gone.

"Sounds good, Prez," he replied. "And I'm here, a thousand fucking percent. But seriously, what the fuck happened while I was gone?"

That pulled a harsh, bitter laugh out of me. "What *didn't* fucking happen? Roadkill kicked up a lot of shit and then Rocky had her crazy gangbanging ex after her, which meant us. You were here for the shit with Vivi, and I'm guessing this current shit show is a combination of Roadkill and something we can't see yet."

"Can't Jag call up his girl to use her magic fingers and help us?"

I shook my head at him. "Sometimes you really are an insensitive prick."

"What?"

"Dude, she's working off *our* time. Don't be an asshole."

"So you won't even consider asking if it means saving the rest of us? I'll talk to Jag."

"Your funeral. I wouldn't suggest it, but I'll make sure we have someone here to wire your jaw shut."

CREATIVELY CRUSHED

"He can fucking try it," Gunnar said with that crazy-eyed grin that told everyone else just what a crazy bastard he was. "Seriously, we can't even ask?"

"Ask what, Gunnar? Do you even know where to start looking? Jag is doing his part and I'm doing mine. Focus on Maisie and doing your job."

"Yes, sir," he said tersely and stood, anger emanating from him but I wasn't fazed.

"Don't be an asshole, Gunnar. You're not the only one with problems around here so maybe fucking act like it. In case you forgot, we almost lost Jana. Who is also raising kids. Oh, and she also has a bun in the oven." That changed his demeanor real quick. "And Moon, the owner of that art store who has nothing to do with RB got her shit shot up. So you being a prick doesn't even faze me."

"You're right, man. Shit, man. I'm just…" His words trailed off, but he didn't need to finish them because I knew exactly what the fuck he refused to say.

Scared for his loved ones. "I know, Gunnar, me too."

He nodded and dropped back down in the chair with a heavy exhale. "You? What the fuck for, from what the cops said, you toasted ol' Vigo but good." He laughed, harder and harder. "Crispy nuggets."

My lips twitched but I refused to laugh. Vigo had it coming but that didn't mean I had to like that shit. "That was a happy accident. What happened last night at Stetson wasn't."

"Didn't realize you were back in the game, man."

I snorted a laugh. "I'm not." I told him all about Dodds fucking with us and putting Katrina in handcuffs.

Gunnar looked stunned, something that I'd rarely seen in the fifteen years I'd known him. "Seriously? A trumped-up ID charge? That's fucked up."

"Tanya handled it, but I need you to tell Jag to look into that motherfucker."

CREATIVELY CRUSHED

"You still don't want to contact Vivi? Seems to me this might have something to do with that former governor from Florida she outed in a most spectacular way." His grin turned scandalous and he rubbed his hands together. "It was a thing of beauty, but something that might have some blowback."

"Yeah. You're probably right. Don't say anything to Jag about this, yet. I need to think." I was on my feet and headed toward the door, keys in hand. I needed to think. A long fucking ride was just what I needed to clear my head and organize my thoughts.

After an hour of driving around the desert, occasionally hopping on the freeway to feel the wind against my skin, I found myself at a place I hadn't been in twenty-seven months.

Lauren's grave.

Chapter Eighteen

Moon

Being back at the shop was nice but that probably had more to do with the fact that I was on the gallery side, where the building was still normal. Pristine. Untouched by violence or the blood of my friend.

Being over here allowed me to enjoy stress-free time during the few hours each week I accepted walk-ins from artists. If I didn't set a specific day and time, I'd never get to interact with customers who stopped in for art supplies and classes, which I surprisingly enjoyed more than this part lately.

Not that I didn't love the local artists who brought me everything from oils and watercolors to sculptures and even painted gourds. I loved them and their passion for art, but the shop drew all walks of life. Hobbyists, aspiring artists, part-timers and students all showed up in my shop. It gave me an outside connection to the world that I needed. Appreciated. Relished.

As the final walk-in hours drew to a close, the chimes above the door sounded and I looked up just as Jana entered with Max behind her, several packages under his big biceps. "Hey guys, what are you doing here?"

Jana stepped up to the wide wooden table with a smile on her face as she rubbed her growing belly. "I figured I wouldn't make you track me down this year, since you saved my life and all."

"While I'm pretty sure that was the doctors, I'm glad you came in of your own free will today. You were giving me a complex," I said as a joke. I knew we were both thinking about Jana from a few years back, so shy and insecure, always hiding the scar on her face that was barely even visible. I hounded her for weeks to be in my art show until she'd relented.

"And now I'm here to make up for it. Hopefully." With a nod to Max, who placed three large paper-covered frames on the table, Jana began to unwrap each of them. "Let me know what you think," she said, her voice shaky and quiet, like the Jana I'd met years ago.

But she did take a step back, giving me space to examine the paintings laid out before me. They were beautiful but different from her usual landscapes and still lifes. The colors were vibrant and emotional, the subjects all human. Her theme was there too, motherhood or maybe the journey of motherhood. Either way it shone through each painting, evoking a visceral reaction of longing and anticipation.

"Okay, when I said let me know, I kind of meant right now." Jana's nervous laugh sounded behind me, but I was too transfixed by the brush strokes, the colors and the always rounded belly just barely in the frame. The mother was always there, always watching but never quite part of the picture.

"It's beautiful," I told her honestly. "All of them are thought-provoking. Stunning." Turning to Jana, I couldn't help but smile. "I know I don't have a right to be, but I am so proud of you Jana."

She blushed prettily and swiped an errant tear from her eye. "Thanks Moon, that means the world to me."

"Does this mean they're all for the show?" There was more hope than question in my voice and Max snickered, feigning innocence when Jana glared at him.

"Yes, it's for the show, and I'm leaving it all up to you. But now, I have something for you."

I was learning that the Reckless Bastards might be big tough guys, but the women they loved were stronger. Tougher. Max picked up another package. This one wasn't framed, and it was even larger than her paintings for the showing. Slowly and carefully I unrolled the cream drawing paper, revealing a variation on gladiator sandals, long legs and a tie-dye bodice. By the time I reached the top there was no mistaking who it was. Me. "As an Amazonian superhero?"

"Exactly what I said," Max added proudly.

CREATIVELY CRUSHED

"It's not a superhero or an Amazonian, Moon, it's you. Just you." She pointed to the hair, long black waves falling of the shoulders and she'd somehow managed to make the streaks of silver shine like diamonds through the sketch.

"I didn't even know you sketched."

"I don't, which makes it a double gift for you. You get my first piece in a new medium, well more like my fifty-first but that part can stay our little secret."

"I'll take it to my grave," I promised. "Seriously Jana, I'm honored. You really are a tremendous artist."

"You should see me work a spreadsheet," she joked, still not completely comfortable with praise.

"I have." Max and I both laughed at the instant flush of her pale ivory skin, barely colored at all from the hot desert sun. "Client, remember?"

"Pregnancy brain, remember?"

"It's been a few years but I do recall you ordered twice as many brushes as I needed and not enough paper. You need omega-3's."

"See Max, I told you Moon would have an answer." She leaned into his affectionate touch and I had to look away. So much love and admiration, respect between the happy couple that I felt a pang of longing for something I wasn't even sure I wanted.

Men had proven a disappointment in the long run so when I happened upon one, I never kept them for very long. It was easier that way. For everyone. A buzzing sounded in the distance and it took me a moment to realize I still had guests inside the gallery.

"Moon are you all right? Did you hear me?" Jana's hand grabbed my shoulder and I looked down at her. "Your phone, it's ringing. Has been for a while," she added with worry in her voice.

"Sorry I must have zoned out for a minute. Excuse me?"

"Take your time."

I hit redial on the unfamiliar number with a frown. "Hello, someone just called from this number?" I was prepared for an unsolicited sales call but I wasn't prepared for the frightened woman on the other end of the line.

"Are you Moon Vanderbilt, Beau's mother?"

Oh God, not Beau. "I am. What's wrong? Please just tell me, no sugarcoating."

"Beau is having an asthma attack, a pretty bad one. His inhaler isn't working and the nurse is unfamiliar with the portable machine in his backpack."

"He needs—"

"An ambulance is already on the way Ms. Vanderbilt. It'll be much faster for you to meet him at the hospital."

My heart raced like I'd just run a marathon and for several seconds, I couldn't breathe. Couldn't focus on anything at all. "Oh. Okay. Thank you, Miss…?"

"Charles. Charlene Charles. Good luck with Beau."

The call ended. I don't know how long before I finally got my feet moving across the gallery and toward the door.

"Beau is having another attack," I explained and tossed the shop keys to Max. "Lock up?"

"We got it. Go take care of my little man," Jana insisted with a worried smile. "Call us if you need anything."

With a brief nod, I pushed through the doors and quickly made the trip back home to pick up my purse and my car but I was brought up short after re-locking the front door. "Cross, what are you doing here?"

"What's wrong?" Big strong hands landed on my shoulders, deep blue eyes looking at me like he was genuinely concerned.

"Nothing. I can't talk, not now." Keys fell from shaky hands but Cross was there picking them up. "Sorry. Thanks. I have to go…Beau."

"What's wrong with Beau?" His question was straightforward but there was tension in his voice like my little boy mattered to him.

"He had another asthma attack at camp today and they called the ambulance. I need to be there when he gets to the hospital."

"Of course you do," he said easily and put one hand against my lower back, guiding me forward as he slipped the keys from my hand. "I'll drive." Cross pulled the passenger door open and nodded for me to get in.

I stared numbly at his delicious backside when he jogged around the front of the car. "You don't have to do this."

"I know I don't. But I'm doing it anyway."

"Thanks." It had been a long time since I had someone to lean on or even to drive me while Beau was in the middle of an attack. "Did you stop by for something, Cross?"

He grinned over at me, blue eyes twinkling. "To see you, Moon."

"Oh." What else could I say?

Chapter Nineteen

Cross

I don't know how in the hell I the designated chaperone for Beau in his hospital room was. But after Moon spoke with the doctor who assured her that Beau wasn't in grave danger, she'd run home to get him a change of clothes. The poor kid had sweated through his own during his ordeal. Now though, two hours later, there was no sign that anything had ever been wrong with the kid, aside from his pale skin. His blue eyes were big and wide, sparkling with excitement.

"What's up, kid?"

He bit his lip, a move his mom often did when she was deep in thought or concentration. "What does your club do? My mom says you're in a motorcycle club."

His words surprised me, not his curiosity, because Beau was smart as hell and twice as curious and interested in every damn thing. What surprised me was that Moon had told him anything about the club *and* that she hadn't called it a gang.

"We own a few businesses together, we ride together and we're friends, though we think of each other as family."

His inky brows dipped into a low vee across his forehead in confusion. "Like me and my mom?"

I nodded and he mimicked my actions.

"I wish we had more family, but Mom says you don't always stay with the family you're born with. Is your club big?"

I couldn't help but wonder what had happened to the family Moon had been born with, because based on the few hints she'd dropped, they were old money and controlling as fuck.

"Pretty big. There are about fifty of us and some of those guys have wives and girlfriends. Kids."

Every year there were more and more women and kids around, which I loved because roots gave a man a reason not to fuck up too bad. But I also hated it

CREATIVELY CRUSHED

because it reminded me of what I didn't have. Likely wouldn't have again.

"Fifty people? Cool!" Beau's big blue eyes were filled with mischief. "Can I meet them?"

I laughed. Beau was a wily character, using his adorable charm to work around his mother. "We'll have to ask your mom."

His bottom lip stuck out in a pout that was more adorable than anything, especially since he didn't seem like a kid prone to tantrums. "Wanna play cards?" he asked.

"Uh, sure. What do you know how to play?"

I hadn't played any kid games since I was a boy myself, and that was too long ago to even consider.

"Can you teach me a game?"

How could I say no to that face? As much as it hurt to be around him and not think about how my own kid would have been, each time we were together, it got easier. "Sure."

Beau handed me the deck of cards and I taught him how to play a man's card game, which was how Moon and Dr. Yang found us.

"Mom, I got a full house!" Beau, already forgetting the importance of secrecy in the game, held his cards up high for the women to see. I folded.

The little boy had gotten me to fold trip Kings. "I'm out."

Beau giggled when Moon came closer, holding her fist up for him to bump. "Good job."

I frowned and sat up. "You're not upset?"

She blinked slowly, her black lashes fanning sensually over cool green eyes. "Well you have given him another game to beat me at, so yeah I'm a little upset. But why would I be upset about poker?"

"Gambling?"

She laughed. "Poker isn't gambling, Cross. If you know how to play it's like driving. You do the best you can with the information you have and you hope all goes well. Sometimes it doesn't."

CREATIVELY CRUSHED

I stared at her for a long time, trying to figure out if she was for real or just doing that thing where women pretend something is okay and then freak out about it later. If she was for real, she was damn near perfect.

"Okay. Good."

Her lips twitched but Moon stayed quiet and turned to the doctor.

Dr. Yang slid a gaze to me, equal parts confused and wary. "Do you want to step out in the hall?"

Moon looked to me and back to the doctor with a casual shake of her head. "No, it's fine. He's a friend."

"He's my friend too," Beau added with a wide grin for me.

"Okay." Dr. Yang didn't seem to mind either way and that made me respect her more. I was used to everyone from cops and doctors, cashiers and every other goddamn person judging me by my tattoos, my *kutte* and my bike.

"It is my strong recommendation that Beau begins the stem cell treatments right away. He's young and this treatment will reduce inflammation and regenerate lung tissue, which will decrease his attacks."

That sounded good to me, but Moon was still in her fierce protector role. "Decrease?"

The doctor smile sympathetically. "As the therapy works it will help reshape Beau's airways and that combined with the reduced inflammation *could* stop them altogether, but you know I can't make that promise. Dr. Mankowski can give you more information."

She kept talking about the procedure and what to expect but Moon wasn't paying attention.

I could tell she was numb. Worried. Afraid. I stood and put my hand on her shoulder. Tension was woven into every fiber of her being, so much that she practically vibrated with it. Beau sensed it and the doctor could see it.

"Anything else, Dr. Yang?" she asked.

The doctor nodded. "I'll let Mankowski know to expect a call from you soon." After looking at Beau's chart and asking him a few questions, Yang jotted down a few notes and left.

Moon sat on the edge of Beau's bed and took his hand. "That doesn't sound so bad, right kiddo?"

He nodded. "Stem cells are like magic, right Mom?"

Moon nodded, still quiet. And still. My heart went out to her and I realized, while Beau tried to make her smile, what my draw to her was beyond her unconventional beauty and the sex. No one could possibly understand my inner turmoil like Moon. She was wound so tight and held herself together as if one moment of relaxation, one moment of belief would tear everything apart.

I knew that feeling all too well.

"So, we're doing this," she said on a rushed breath that made me and Beau smile.

"Yep, we are, Mom."

My phone buzzed, and I hated to intrude on this moment with real life shit, but I couldn't ignore it.

Pulling it out, I took a quick glance at the screen and groaned at the message from Jag.

Roadkill is behind the donations. Find me when you get back.

Shit. I had to go.

"What's up?" Moon asked casually.

"I have to go. Something's come up."

Moon stood and turned to me, those green eyes looking all the way to the deepest part of me. Deliberately. "Go take care of business. If you want, we're having dinner at seven."

"We're having mashed potatoes, right Mom?"

I smiled and winked at the kid. "I love mashed potatoes."

"Me too and Mom puts all kind of stuff in it. You'll like it."

And how could I resist an invitation like that? "I'll be there." With a quick kiss to Moon's cheek, I took

CREATIVELY CRUSHED

long strides out of the hospital and called one of the prospects to come pick me up.

***

"We ready to do this?" I stood by my bike and looked around at the men who had come with me to find White Boy Craig. Stitch, Golden Boy, Savior and Jag had offered to come with me and there was no way in hell I'd do this without them.

"Fuck yeah," Savior growled. "I should be at home licking chocolate off my woman's sexy body so yeah, I'm ready to fuck some shit up."

The rest of the men nodded. None of us were eager to do what had to be done, but we'd all served in the military which meant we were all well versed in doing what the fuck needed to be done. "I just want answers."

"And if we can't get them?" Golden Boy wore that psycho smile he'd worn before his prison days. It was intimidating as hell, but more than that, he was capable of following through, probably even more now that he had a wife and kid to look after.

"If we don't get them the easy way, we'll get answers the hard way."

It was exactly what they wanted to hear. We were all sick of the constant bullshit lately. The problems with the city were fucking with our businesses, which made this shit personal. Roadkill had gone after our club and our women and nothing was more fucking personal than that.

My gaze connected with each man, making sure we were all on the same page as we rounded the brick façade and strode into the all-wood bar, *Shandy's*.

It looked like one of those old school saloons, complete with swinging doors after the bouncer checked ID's. I passed the long pine bar with the brass foot rest, nodding to the old bartender, Tiki, as I passed. Tiki was a big ass motherfucker who didn't take any shit and didn't like trouble inside his bar.

CREATIVELY CRUSHED

The tables were filled with men and women drinking and playing cards or dominoes while a few of the tables were filled with couples trying not to get caught by husbands and wives.

"In the back." I said the words over my shoulder, pointing so Golden Boy and Savior saw.

White Boy Craig sat at the big table in the back surrounded by a few other members of Roadkill MC, plus the same blonde from Moon's shop. Pacheco's daughter. Craig's laughter died when he caught sight of us, but it was quickly replaced with his trademark sneer.

"Well what do we have here? You boys come to celebrate?"

"Yeah, but we forgot the barbecue sauce to pour out in memory of Vigo." Savior was never one to back away from a challenge and his words hit their mark.

White Boy Craig was on his feet and in my face. "What did you say?" he growled, though he had to look up at me because I had a few inches on the scrawny motherfucker.

"Don't mind Savior," I said. "Everyone knows you need ketchup or A1 sauce when the meat is well done." I tried like hell to keep my mouth in a straight line but the outrage on his face made it difficult. "Now do you want to fight and risk Tiki's bat to the head or do you wanna go outside and talk, Prez to Prez?"

I knew he'd choose to go outside because despite what they'd tried to do to Mandy, Roadkill was filled with a bunch of sissies. They weren't fighters. That was why they picked on the weaker ones and also why we were all in this shit right now.

"Fine, let's go outside. Stay here," he ordered his men when they gathered behind him. But Lu, the treasurer and the one banging Pacheco's daughter, moved to follow him.

"You sure?" Lu said.

CREATIVELY CRUSHED

"I am," Craig said in a voice that sounded the opposite of sure, but he turned on his heels and walked out of *Shandy's*.

"Okay, Cross, what the fuck do you want?" His arms were crossed over his chest defensively, but I noticed he kept at least six feet of space between us.

"What I want is answers. You still working with the feds?"

His response was immediate and as angry as I expected. "Fuck you."

I shook my head and gave him a disgusted look. "I shouldn't be surprised though. One snitch usually lives in a den of 'em."

"Fuck you."

"No thanks, White Boy. You ain't my type. I'm sure you'll be someone's bitch when you get to prison."

He leapt toward me, hands out like a fucking baby just learning how to walk. I sidestepped him, grabbing his throat and pushing him up against *Shandy's* back wall.

"You fucking cowards are really in the pocket of a fucking local politician with no power?" It was still hard to believe that a bunch of bumbling idiots had stumbled into this shit. There had to be more to it.

"Shows what you know," he said, grabbing at my hands that still held a tight grip on his throat. "Pacheco is headed for the big time. He's on the shortlist for senator."

I laughed so hard I nearly loosened my damn grip on this fool's throat. "You can't really be that dumb, can you?"

"Fuck you," he spat at me but I was still laughing because not only was Roadkill filled with dumbasses, but they had no clue who they were involved with. "What the fuck do you know?"

"More than you, apparently. We already have two senators, both re-elected in the past four years, so if you can't count, that means Pacheco ain't gonna be shit. You got played." And that was almost satisfying considering all the trouble we'd had thanks to these assholes. "So fucking played."

CREATIVELY CRUSHED

"You're wrong. That governor who got taken down means they need another one." Craig insisted. "Pacheco will be that man."

"He was from another state, dumbass. Pacheco is probably pocketing all that money you funneled his way." That tidbit shocked Craig into silence and I barked out a laugh. I couldn't believe these guys were that stupid.

"Get your fuckin' hands off my Prez." I turned at the sound of Lu's voice. I knew that scratchy smoker's voice well. "Or I'll make you."

"You and what Army? Or did you bring a step ladder so you can reach me?"

Craig took his moment to swing, narrowly missing me but his fist grazed my jaw and I pressed my thumb into the beating pulse at the base of his throat.

Lu lunged forward but in an act of disrespect, Jag grabbed the back of his shirt and damn near lifted him off the ground.

"I don't think so, Lu. Don't make me embarrass you in front of your girl." Jag's voice was low and deep. Menacing. Badass.

Damn! I loved my brother.

"I'll fucking kill you, Jag." Lu said.

"You can try," he said even quieter than before. "But you'll bleed out before you get to that blade in your back pocket or that piece under your *kutte*."

"Everybody calm the fuck down!" I called out. I took a step away from Craig but kept my hand on his throat, applying pressure just because I could. "Craig here was telling me that Pacheco will be our next junior Senator from Nevada. You boys believe that?"

The Reckless Bastards laughed and I continued, "Unlike these dumb sons of bitches, we know the only way to change the system is to understand how it works."

"Someone ought to tell him it's too late and his name isn't on any ballot," Jag said on a laugh as he let Lu go with a shove.

CREATIVELY CRUSHED

Pacheco's daughter went to Lu and I knew this was my moment to cause a little drama because I had the upper hand.

"You're Pacheco's daughter, Carly, is it?"

"Yeah. You got a problem with that?"

"No, I'm just curious how much extra money they threw to your old man just to get your sweet ass as part of their deal."

Lu stiffened, and Carly took a step away from him. "What are you talking about?"

"Don't listen to a word he says, babe. His whole club is full of fucking liars." Lu moved in and wrapped an arm around her, pressing his lips to the spot behind her ear.

"You mean I'm lying when your own Prez already confirmed you've been funneling a fuck ton of money to Pacheco's nonexistent Senate campaign? I wonder what that money is for if not his campaign."

"Daddy isn't running for Senate. He's retiring when his term is up." Her wide eyes bounced between me and Lu, conflicted and angry. "What's he talking about Lu?"

"Yeah, Lu. You're the MC treasurer. Tell your girl what I'm talking about, unless you want me to show her?"

That did it. Carly took three big steps away from Lu, as clear a 'fuck you' as any words could ever be. "No! Don't fucking touch me!"

"Tell her about the money, Lu."

"Shut the fuck up, Cross!"

I smiled. "I have no beef with you, sweetheart. I'm just trying to figure out why the city is doing this asshole's dirty work."

"Maybe you should run your businesses better, you piece of shit," White Boy Craig spat out.

Craig choked and grabbed my wrist as I squeezed harder and harder until his face turned red. There was no anger in me, just a cool calm certainty that I could kill this asshole in a split second if I wanted to.

CREATIVELY CRUSHED

"That's rich coming from an asshole who got conned out of millions," Savior added, swinging a punch at a Roadkill newbie who got in his face. "Funny how you know so much about *our* business when you got fucked out of so much money."

"You're wrong," Craig insisted, but all the fire was gone.

"I have proof. In fact, my guess is that you guys are working for Pacheco, and he asked you to keep an eye on his precious little girl. And you sent her in to the shop to check up on things, am I right?" I turned my attention to Carly. "Did these goons have you do that? Does your father know what an upstanding citizen you are? Trying to scare a single mom and her son?"

Carly slapped Lu across the face and backed up. "You asshole! I can't believe you work for my father! You're just like the rest. The same loser ass kissers that follow him everywhere. Fuck you, Lu! I'm so outta here!" She stalked off, giving each and every one of us a peek at her perky twenty-one-year-old ass nearly poking out of her jean shorts.

"Thanks dude," she tossed off in a huff, "whoever you are!"

"No problem, sweetheart," I shot back. She was a feisty little thing but that also meant within the hour Pacheco would know he was compromised. I turned to my prey. "So White Boy, what's your end game?"

He grinned, coughing when I squeezed just a little harder. "Wait and see, asshole."

"See, I try to be nice but you just push and push." My voice was low and calm, no longer determined to be a nice guy. I pulled my elbow back and unleashed a powerful punch that made a sickening crack as it landed on his nose, sending his head against the wall. When I let him go, Craig slid to the ground.

His guys surged forward but they weren't quick enough. My guys were on them in a flash.

"Whoa boy!" Savior flashed his wide-eyed psycho grin and sent a fist flying into the nearest Roadkill member. "We got us a good old-fashioned street fight!"

CREATIVELY CRUSHED

It was an all-out fucking fight; Reckless Bastards against Roadkill MC and it had been coming for a long time.

Craig made it to his feet when I wasn't looking and swung at me. I ducked that shit and sent my fist right into his stomach, grabbing the back of his neck when he staggered back. I twisted his head and smashed his face into the wall. "If this was real brick you'd be dead. Just think about that, asshole."

He grunted and held his bleeding nose, not bothering to look up at me. "You got me now, Cross, but you fuckers better enjoy these days because they will be your last."

I laughed and spit on that piece of shit before I lifted my hand like it was a gun and pulled the imaginary trigger. "Right back atcha, motherfucker."

I walked away and took a moment to stare at my men, happily pounding away on just a few of the assholes making our lives difficult at the moment.

"All right boys let's get the fuck outta here!"

Each one got another punch or kick in before stepping back with wide, shit-eating grins. "Got the fightin' part of the evenin' out the way, now I'm ready for food and fuckin'!" Savior smacked his hands together and whooped loudly, making us all smile.

"Good night assholes." I walked away, White Boy Craig's angry words hitting my back and bouncing right off. Now that I knew what the deal was, I could plan our retaliation.

Jag came up beside me. "Feel better?"

"Fuck no."

I didn't feel good about any of this because it wasn't the end, just the beginning. And before this shit with Roadkill and Pacheco was over, some of us would be hurt. Or dead.

"You?" I asked.

Jag looked grim. "Won't feel better until Vivi's back in my arms."

"At least you have a woman waiting to come back to you."

CREATIVELY CRUSHED

I didn't mean for it to sound bitter, but I was. Each one of my men was headed home to women who loved them, and although I could get a piece of ass when needed, I was headed back to the only place that was home to me.

The Reckless Bastards clubhouse.

Alone.

KB WINTERS

Chapter Twenty

Moon

I had a date that night. With Cross. Jana claimed she was missing Beau, which I believed, but not more than her desire to play matchmaker. When she'd taken Beau and his backpack filled with games, snacks, pajamas and a clean outfit, I took advantage and texted Cross a dinner invite. Dinner *was* on the menu, I'd just put a casserole in the oven about five minutes ago, but Cross was the entrée as far as I was concerned. It wasn't often—okay it was never—that I got a night like this to enjoy a man and I planned to enjoy it. Even if it was just another night of crazy sexy bliss.

It was enough.

The doorbell rang and my breath caught, which shocked me. Nervous. I was nervous about spending an unsupervised evening with a man. Not just any man though. *Cross.* He of the searing deep blue eyes and kissable mouth. And that tattoo-covered body appealed to the artist in me like nothing else ever had.

Checking my reflection one last time, I didn't recognize the woman staring back at me. Her long salt and pepper hair was fuller and shinier than mine, her green eyes shimmered like emeralds compared to the minty green color of my own. But most of all, the woman staring back at me emanated a sensuality I had never possessed other than in action.

Sex had always come easily but it had been a long time since I'd felt sensual. Or sexy.

"You gonna open the door or do I have to whisper some magic code to get inside?"

His voice shouldn't have startled me on the other side of the door, but I was too lost in my own thoughts and concerns. I took a deep breath and blew it out as I walked to the door and smoothed the long green dress I'd worn tonight. For Cross. I opened the door and asked, "Do you *know* the magic code?"

CREATIVELY CRUSHED

His lips quirked into a lopsided grin as his heated gaze raked over my body and made me wish I'd worn a bra. "I know the code, Moon. You look...fucking delicious."

Cross looked beyond delicious tonight in a pair of light-colored jeans that hugged his thighs like a cowboy. I couldn't wait to see his fine backside. He wore one of those long-sleeved t-shirts that made his already delicious muscles drool-worthy. My only complaint was that it covered up his beautiful art, though I planned to see it all.

Later.

"I'll take it. Come on in." I stepped back and sure, maybe it was a tad bit creepy, but I breathed in his scent. Long and deep until it was in my lungs and my brain. Every part of me. "You smell good," I said, unable to hide my smile.

He grinned back and cut a look at me from the corner of his eyes. "Thanks."

"What happened?" I pushed the door closed and locked it before turning back to Cross and the bruise forming on his jaw.

"Nothing worth mentioning. I'd rather talk about you in this dress."

"I'll let you get away with that. For now, and only because I smell sugar in that bag." I didn't eat refined sugar nearly as much as I wanted to and right now I didn't know if it was Cross or the sugar making me salivate.

"Sugar and booze."

"Magic words to these ears." I turned my back to him and signaled him to follow me into the kitchen. I felt his eyes burn through the back of my dress. It was held together in back by nothing but a series of intricate straps.

"Damn, I love that dress."

I turned around at that. "Thanks. It's new." I suddenly felt like a school girl on her first date, blushing at every little compliment. "What's in the bag?"

"Wouldn't you like to know?" Cross licked his lips, eyes never leaving mine as he pulled the items from his bag.

Finally, I broke the intense stare before I lost all control and stripped down and spread across the countertop, begging Cross to have his way with me. My lips curved up. "You brought the blueberry wine!"

"It's the canna-wine. And dairy-free pastries, in case there are any left over and Beau wants some."

Was it possible for ovaries to explode? Because I was pretty sure that low vibrating hum in my body was the sound of my ovaries preparing for detonation. "Are you going to have any?"

"Why not? Your food usually sounds a bit weird but so far you haven't let my taste buds down. Not even once." His smile grew wider when his words gave me a shiver. "Dirty girl."

"Because that's not what you meant?" He shrugged and I rolled my eyes as I reached for the wine. "Aside from the mystery bruise, how are things?"

"Good. Still up in the air. You?"

Okay, so he didn't want to talk. "Fine." I poured the wine and slid a glass to him before raising my own. "To keeping things good and fair, now and forevermore."

"Forevermore?"

I shrugged. "What? I'm feeling a bit poetic tonight. Just wait until the wine kicks in."

"I look forward to it." Finally, Cross tapped his glass against mine and we both drank the wine. It was cool and delicious with just a hint of pot flavor.

I drank more than half the glass and grinned up at Cross. "Delicious. Hungry yet?"

"Starved," he said and I knew he wasn't talking about the casserole I'd put in the oven. The way his gaze lingered like a caress all over my body was intoxicating all on its own, the wine only giving everything a radiant tint that was almost dreamlike.

"Dinner won't be ready for another thirty-five minutes."

"That's plenty of time."

I knew what he was thinking but I really wanted to hear him say it. "For?"

Cross drained the rest of his glass and pulled me close. My chest heaved and blood flowed through me, hot and thick, like lava.

"This," he hissed.

Then his lips were on mine, demanding and insistent as they slicked across my lips, top and then bottom and back to top. Teasing and tasting my mouth like it was a magnificent feast fit for a king. I was too far gone to resist, too far gone to do anything other than take it. Absorb the heat and passion he transferred from his big strong body to mine.

There was something different about this kiss. It was almost surreal the way his kisses took me out of my body and carried me off on a cloud of lust and need. Want.

"Cross," I moaned when he broke the kiss, blinking to clear the fog from my brain but nope, he was still there looking good enough to eat.

His blue eyes were so dark they may as well have been black but when his lips melted into a smile, my legs buckled just a little.

"This time, I'm fuckin' you on a bed."

Why those words sent another shiver through me, I couldn't say. But this version of Cross tonight was darker and grittier, hungry with a raw need that was one hundred percent focused on me.

"Oh, okay."

He grinned, like he was satisfied with the effect he was having on me and scooped me up in his arms like I was one of those dainty women that men always carried around simply because they could.

"The correct answer is, 'Yes, Cross'."

I laughed and licked his neck up to his jaw line. "Yes, Cross."

I couldn't help it, I inhaled his scent at the crook of his neck and shivered as it hit my nostrils. I craved his scent more than I realized.

"Fuck, that's hot." Cross was on a mission and I was his target but rather than being scared, I was thrilled. Turned on. Inside my bedroom he tossed me on the bed and then turned on all the lights.

"Stay right there," he ordered.

I was about to sit up and take my off my clothes but then Cross began to undress. I was transfixed by the sight of all that flesh, all those muscles on display, bunching and flexing with every move he made.

"Yes, Cross," I said again, just to get another rise out of him. But this time the rise was growing longer and thicker by the second behind those blue and white striped boxer briefs. I licked my lips at the sight he made.

"I feel overdressed."

He grinned and knelt on the bed. "Let's see."

Cross pushed up the fabric of my dress to my knees and stopped. "How dressed are you?"

His hands slid up my thighs, warm and slightly rough, making me shiver. "Panties. Too bad."

"I wore them for you." My legs parted just a little, enough to make him groan.

"Yeah?"

I nodded, and a wide, satisfied smile crossed his face as he dipped under the skirt of my dress and put his mouth on me.

He didn't even bother to remove my panties, just licked and sucked my pussy through the silk.

"Oh, Cross!"

His wide shoulders pushed my thighs further apart as his tongue licked my clit, my lips and he sucked hard and then soft. In little soft pulsing sucking motions and harder, slurping motions. It was fantastic.

CREATIVELY CRUSHED

It was too much pleasure at once, but I never wanted it to end.

Then he sat up and ripped off my panties, pulled my dress off over my head and I was completely naked. Bared to him.

"Mine," he growled and settled between my legs again, this time his mouth moved with a ferocity I couldn't resist. Hard and fast, he licked and sucked, nibbled and laved every inch of me until my body shook with the undeniable need for orgasm.

"Cross, please."

I didn't know what I was begging for other than more of him. I didn't want it to stop but I felt the orgasm start in my toes. "Yes! Oh, yes!"

The room was silent aside from my moans and cries, and the completely erotic sound of Cross's mouth bringing me to the brink of ecstasy. I should have been embarrassed about how wet I was, but Cross seemed turned on by it considering the intensity of his mouth on me.

"Oh!" I kept moaning, over and over.

While his mouth made love to my body, I floated on the air above us, watching with a wild fascination I couldn't explain. Then he slipped one finger between my cheeks into that forbidden hole where only his tongue had been before.

I shouldn't like it.

It felt strange. Overwhelming.

Wickedly delicious.

"Oh, oh Cross!" My body was on fire but not like a regular old building fire, no, this was like a explosives warehouse had been set on fire by an arsonist. This was a thousand alarm fire inside of me, a raging inferno that shot out of me with my orgasm, threatening to burn everything and everyone within a ten-mile radius.

"Yes!"

I grabbed his head and rode his face, grinding my ass on his finger until my whole body twisted and curled into the most powerful orgasm of my life.

CREATIVELY CRUSHED

"Damn, Moon," he said when he finally eased himself up.

He licked his lips, staring at me with a smile slick with my juices.

"I think that's my line." He smiled again and brushed a kiss to my lips so I could taste myself on his tongue. "Delicious."

"Now I know *that* was my line." He kissed me again, long and hard and with complete confidence in skill, which he'd more than earned. He kissed me until I was breathless and clinging to his wide, muscular back. In too much of a hurry to be buried where I needed him the most, Cross didn't bother to remove his boxers, he just shoved them down until all the best parts were uncovered.

My legs wrapped around him as soon as he did that, urging him closer to where my body still pulsed for him.

"That was incredible," I cried, pleading for more.

He laughed and lined our bodies up before he thrust in so slow my moan came out long and low.

"You feel incredible. Fuck, your pussy is always so damn wet. Is that all for me?"

"I don't know, is it? Oh!"

His hips pushed forward to *that spot*, the one that made smart women stupid for another press of that erotic button. Over and over he hit that spot until another orgasm, forceful and fast, shot through me.

"Cross!"

But he didn't let up, not this time. His blue eyes glazed over and took on that faraway look as they stared deep into my soul. He reared up on his knees and flung my thighs over his so I was spread wide while he watched.

"Moon, look at me." When I did, Cross licked his thumb and pressed it to my clit.

"Fuck, yeah," he groaned when I quivered and pulsed around him. "Fuck. Your pussy is so good."

I loved his dirty talk. It was raw and dirty, not polite. Not PC. Just raw, hot and nasty.

"God, Cross. I need more." My nails dug into his shoulders and he didn't seem to care, which only ratcheted up my desire even more.

He growled at my words and let one hand slide up the center of my body, leaving a trail of heat I couldn't ignore. Then his hand was at my throat and though I knew I should have been scared, I wasn't. Not when his big hand wrapped around me with just enough pressure to be scary.

"Blueberry wine. You like it," he said when I pulsed around him again. And again.

"Maybe," I whispered, teasing him until he applied a bit more pressure. With that pressure came another surge of his cock, long and thick and hard, I felt him deep inside of me. He filled me up good, choking me while he fucked me hard, making me feel like the dirty girl I'd never been.

"No, that's what you say if you want me to stop. Blueberry wine."

"Oh." I licked my lips and nodded. "Got it." I put my inner muscles to work, squeezing him tight and loving the way his eyes slammed closed against the force of his own desire.

"Oh shit, babe."

Harder and harder he thrust into me, long sure strokes that kept me on the wrong side of my next orgasm, which I was pretty sure might kill me anyway.

"Fucking hell, Moon!"

"Yes!" I could barely get the word out but I wasn't worried. Not yet anyway. "Cross!"

"I need you to come for me one more time, Moon. We're on the clock, remember?"

That made me smile, which was pretty incredible since I was sure my body was ten seconds away from total combustion. His other hand went to my clit and pinched, and that was the push I needed to jump off the building and float in a slow sweeping motion, only vaguely aware of the man on top of me, thrusting deeply with his face twisted in sweet, beautiful agony.

"Whoa!"

A rush of liquid between my thighs spread out in a warm pool between us and if I had been thinking about it, I might have felt some kind of embarrassment but I felt too good to care.

A grin split his mouth but his hips never stopped moving, pounding harder and deeper into me until I felt it, that moment he thickened and grew harder inside me.

"Oh fuck, Moon! Ah, Moon!" Head thrown back as his hips thrust into me one final time, he looked beautiful.

At peace.

Then his big sweaty body fully covered mine the way his lips did, kissing me long and slow with emotion I knew shouldn't be real, but it felt real and, in that moment, with my body so spent and my mind so open, I couldn't tell the difference.

And when he pulled back with that sexy, lazy smile, I knew I was in trouble.

I had it bad for Cross.

Which was bad.

Really bad.

Chapter Twenty-One

Cross

"I've been peeling back the layers of these fucking shell corporations, which means Roadkill has a damn good accountant working for them."

Jag shook his head in disbelief as he stood in my office trying to explain how he unraveled the Roadkill shit show. "They've given millions to a political action committee that supports Pacheco, but most of the money came in before there was a campaign. The money goes back more than a year but the PAC was formed officially about ten weeks ago."

Which made no fucking sense because Pacheco was a big fish in a very little, local pond. He didn't need a goddamn PAC and definitely not one with millions of dollars in it.

"Fuck. How in the hell does Roadkill pull down that kind of fucking cash?"

"Exactly. I'm still digging into each of the corporations to find out what the fuck else they're into. I've seen their businesses and they're not even pulling in what we are annually." Jag's face showed the same disbelief I was sure mine did.

"They're into some big shit. Have to be." Nothing else made any sense. "How long will it take you to find more?"

Jag shrugged. "Depends on how much more information is available, but I'll need a few days."

"In the meantime, I want you to reach out to a blogger. Someone small enough to stay under the radar but big enough that the story might catch the attention of a bigger outlet."

A slow smile lit up his face, the first genuine smile I'd seen since Vivi left.

"Yeah, I know the perfect person."

We stood at the same time and joined the rest of the guys in the main room of the clubhouse. Jag dropped into a seat and flipped open his laptop, fingers flying over the keyboard to do what I asked.

"Girls, we need some privacy."

There were always a few Reckless Bitches hanging around, but the number had dwindled after one of them targeted Golden Boy's woman, Teddy. They were back now but they knew club business was strictly private.

"Thanks, girls."

"What's up, Cross?" Golden Boy stood, already on alert, and looked at me with a frown.

"A lot."

I didn't sugarcoat shit with my men, especially now that they had wives and kids to worry about. They needed to know what the fuck was going on and what kind of danger we faced.

"Jag came through again with a shit ton of information."

I told them everything I'd learned about the connection between Pacheco and Roadkill.

"Jag hasn't found proof yet, but it seems like this isn't just about campaign promises, it seems like he's a goddamn honorary member of Roadkill MC. I don't want to pull the trigger, yet, but we need to apply some fucking pressure. Let them know no one gets away with fucking with the Reckless Bastards."

"Goddamn right!" Savior smacked the table and a bunch of guys joined in, whooping and hooting. Ready for war.

"That means we need to prepare."

"And retaliate," Max said, his voice deadly cool.

"Max is right, Cross. We can't let these fuckers get away with this shit. Who knows what they'll do next." Golden Boy dropped a hand on his brother's shoulder in solidarity.

"I know. That's why I need you two to round up all the women, including any Reckless Bitches who're in town. Moon too," I told them, ignoring the surprised looks and smirks from my men. "Get them here and keep them here until we know the danger has passed. Be fast about it, the prospects and the Bitches will get them anything else they need.

Max and Golden Boy nodded, grabbed their weapons and left quickly. This wasn't the first time we'd been on lockdown and it probably wouldn't be the last. We knew how to handle it but now there were more women and children to deal with.

"Stitch, I need you to go pick up Tanya. Brief her on the way back here."

He grinned because he was sweet on our attorney. "Sure thing, Prez."

"Me and Lasso will go prep weapons."

Despite being a moody bastard, Savior was a reliable member. And it helped that he fucking loved his weapons.

"Yeah, thanks." The guys all had their assignments and those that didn't were busy getting things ready for the arrival of the women and a long wait. I hoped it wouldn't be too long, because we had all the evidence we needed to fuck up Pacheco's and Roadkill's worlds.

Stitch showed up followed by Tanya breezing in on her ridiculously high heels, which, as usual, she paired with jeans and a button up blouse she tied at the waist. Stitch couldn't keep his eyes off her but she was oblivious.

"All right, Cross. What's so important that I had to pass *Zumbo's Just Desserts* and come straight to your playhouse?" Her pink lips twitched when several of the men frowned in her direction but otherwise she remained unfazed.

"Clubhouse," I corrected with a smirk. "Come over here and Jag and I will brief you." She strolled over, removing a note pad from her bag along with a tablet.

"Okay, what's up?"

"We found some large donations from Roadkill to Pacheco, but they started long before this account was registered to his PAC."

CREATIVELY CRUSHED

Jag nodded and finally looked up from his laptop. "If you look closely," he told Tanya and handed her a flash drive, "you can see that the amounts look like payments. I can't say for what, yet, but it looks like these are payments to a business partner."

Tanya whistled. "Damn, when you boys get into some shit, you get in to the deepest of shit." She shook her head as my words sank in but then like the professional she was, Tanya started taking notes.

"These fuckers fight dirty, Tanya. Really fucking dirty, so we need you briefed on all of this, every damn detail, in case shit goes sideways."

For the next hour she sat beside Jag and listened carefully as he explained every damn thing we had on Pacheco and Roadkill. So far.

Lasso and Savior came back in and Savior nodded to let me know they'd taken care of arming everyone. "We got some knuckles and blades for the guys who can't be strapped," Lasso said with a smile.

At Tanya's look, I shrugged. "We pay attention when you tell us shit."

"Color me surprised," she shot back with a smile and turned her attention back to Jag.

The guys all gravitated towards Savior and Lasso, eager to take their pick of the weapons. They knew this fight would be dirty and they were all ready, because we were always ready. Soldiers, no matter what uniform they wore, never got over being battle-ready at any moment.

Looking around at this group of men who were the only family I had, I couldn't help but worry about some of them. Hell, some of *us*. With that kind of money on the line, there was no telling what they would do to prevent this information from coming to light.

Luckily that was no longer an option.

Finally, the best part of us had arrived. Rocky, Jana and Teddy all sat at one table, looking pregnant and surrounded by the next generation of Bastards. Mandy had just walked in looking tired and all grown up with two large boxes of what had to be her delicious pastries inside. The sound of children grew louder and I scanned for a familiar head capped with black hair.

He wasn't there, and neither was his mother. "Where the fuck is Moon and Beau?"

"She wasn't at home or her shop," Max said with a grunt. He looked as upset as I felt so there was no point in yelling.

"Keep everyone here. I'll be back." I had to find them. Moon knew there was trouble, but she didn't realize she was part of the trouble now. I couldn't let anything happen to them.

Not again.

Chapter Twenty-Two

Moon

"Mom, I feel weird." Beau's voice came out shaky but that wasn't what alarmed me. It was that low whistling wheeze that left me terrified.

"Weird how, honey? Talk slowly and tell me what you're feeling." His voice quivered with fear, the same fear that snaked its way down my spine as soon as his breaths started coming in tight and unusually constricted, like his chest was in a vise. We were on our way to see Dr. Mankowski for the first stem cell treatment and I had no idea where the closest hospital was, so I stomped on the gas to get to the specialist's office as soon as possible.

"It hurts, Mom. I can't breathe."

"Okay, baby, hang on. Okay?" With one hand on the wheel, my free hand searched my purse for the portable nebulizer, sending a wish into the universe that it was fully charged.

"Got it! Here you go, honey. Just breathe slowly, Beau, like we practiced."

I breathed in and out slowly until Beau's breathing matched mine.

His little hands took the nebulizer and double-checked all the settings. I checked it every morning after taking it off the charger and each night when I set it to charge but the routine was for him to make sure everything worked. When Beau was satisfied the settings were correct and that his medicine was inserted properly, he inserted the nebulizer into his mouth. After several deep inhales, the wheezing eased but it didn't stop.

"We're just two exits away from Dr. Mankowski's office, Beau. Just stay calm." The words were more for my benefit than Beau's, because as calm as I was on the outside, I felt like a rabid squirrel on the inside.

CREATIVELY CRUSHED

Beau's eyes were wide with the effort to breathe normally.

I may have broken a few traffic laws during the last stretch of road. By the time I turned into the medical center parking lot, Beau's breathing had turned erratic and wheezy again.

"Mom," he gasped, and I slammed on the brakes right in the middle of a row of parking spots, stepped out with my bag and ran around to the backseat, pulling Beau out and running inside the office building with him in my arms.

"Mom," he wheezed again and I nearly fell to my knees.

"It's okay, honey. Just breathe in and out slowly and let me take care of the rest."

I ran as fast as I could through the automatic glass doors, glaring at the nice receptionist for no other reason than I needed her to take me seriously. "I need to see Dr. Mankowski now!"

She smiled that kind but blank look commonly found with receptionists around the world and shook her head. "I'm sorry Miss but this isn't a hospital."

"Don't you think I know that? I have an appointment today and my son had an asthma attack on our way here so get the doctor now or I will skin you alive with my bare hands. Go!"

"I'm sorry ma'am, but—"

"Go! Now!" I wouldn't be so rude normally but this woman was really getting under my skin.

Dr. Mankowski stepped out of a door with a frown marring his boyishly handsome face. He capped off the Steven Martin look with distressed denim under his white doctor's coat. "What's all the commotion?"

"Your receptionist was just telling me that you don't treat emergencies here and that I should find a hospital while my little boy can't breathe."

As expected, the doctor frowned at the perky brunette as he strode over to me. He leaned over to Beau, who was half out of it from struggling to breathe.

CREATIVELY CRUSHED

"What seems to the problem, Beau?" he said in his calm, doctor voice.

Beau raised his head, sleepy blue eyes barely open. "Can't breathe, Dr. Mank."

He grinned and relieved me of my son's weight. "Let's take a look and see if there's something we can do." I followed behind him on wooden legs, wondering if this would ever end. Would there ever come a time when I wouldn't have to worry if the next breath would be his last?

I stood with my head resting on the door while the doctor listened to his lungs. "Is there more I can do to stop these attacks?"

"You're doing everything you can, Ms. Vanderbilt. There is no magic treatment when it comes to asthma. Today the problem is this," he told me, holding the nebulizer up between two fingers.

"These things are great until they aren't. They may as well be disposable because if the batteries aren't perfectly charged, it won't dispense medications evenly."

A rush of fury raced through me. "So today's attack was the fault of the stupid treatment?"

He grinned a smile that lit up his whole face, shaving at least a decade off his face. "Exactly."

"How can that be? That nebulizer is supposed to be state of the art. Why even bother? Can't they make these things infallible?"

Dr. Mankowski removed a prescription pad from the pocket of his lab coat and scribbled on it. "I'll give you a prescription for another, top of the line portable nebulizer just in case, but I'm hoping you won't need it soon."

"And this one isn't going to fail? Is it any better?" I was beyond frustrated. I took the prescription from the doctor and stuffed it in my bag. "So, does that mean we're still doing the stem cell treatment today—or not?"

CREATIVELY CRUSHED

"Yes, we are. As long as you don't mind waiting so we can monitor Beau for a while."

I shook my head because I would wait as long as I had to if it meant Beau would get better. "Of course."

The doctor left us in the waiting room and I couldn't help but think about all the things I'd done to protect Beau from the ravages of asthma. We both ate a whole food, plant-based diet to limit his exposure to allergens, made sure he did deep breathing exercises to strengthen his lungs and airways. I even kept plants in the house to provide clean oxygen. So far none of it had worked to cure him of this disease, and I felt like a failure.

It was bad enough that failure was a common occurrence for all single parents, but to feel like I'd contributed to his pain somehow was worse and I fell into a well of self-pity. Even when they wheeled him into a sterile room for the treatment an hour later, I was still beating myself up. Not just over Beau, either.

When it came to Cross, I was afraid I was falling back into old habits. Beau had been conceived during a wild and wicked weekend spent with the wrong kind of man. I decided then to get over my obsession with bad boys, which effectively meant I'd given up on men.

Until now.

Until I decided to fall for a man who was all wrong for me in so many ways, starting with the fact that he was still in love with his wife. His dead wife. Of course, he hadn't told me so in so many words. But he didn't have to.

Overhearing Cross tell Beau about his lost family answered so many questions for me. His retreat whenever I tried to pry any information from him; his disappearance after our super-heated sexy sessions in bed. That was all he wanted from me. And I'd been so lonely, I willingly fell into his arms whenever he showed up on my doorstep. It was a lose-lose situation for me, which meant it was time to get my head on straight and stop thinking like a silly little girl.

The same thing Daddy had always accused me of being.

CREATIVELY CRUSHED

***

By the time we left Dr. Mankowski's office, the sun had long ago set and the sky was clear yet dark save for the large face of the moon splashing light on the road. Beau was asleep in the back seat, not at all restricted by the seatbelt I'd fastened him into.

The doctor claimed that I would start seeing improvements in Beau's breathing soon and I was hopeful. Not expectant but hopeful, anyway. We would come back in six weeks just to do a checkup and—fingers crossed—see evidence that the treatments were working.

Soft strains of classic rock played on the radio and I tried to hum quietly but inside the quiet car it felt a lot louder than a hum. Still, the sounds of Creedence Clearwater Revival helped calm my nerves.

At least until the single light of the motorcycle's headlight moved behind me and stayed there for more than ten miles. Initially I thought, okay I hoped it was Cross because he was so eager to see and kiss me again. Then I told myself to stop fantasizing that life was like a romance novel. I kept driving, but still the bike stayed behind me, never allowing more than one car between us. Then the hair on my arms and the back of my neck stood up, a clear sign that something was wrong. I'd learned never to ignore those feelings and signs a long time ago, so I decided to test my theory.

I slowed down and instead of going around me like any normal driver would, he slowed too. When I switched lanes, the biker did too and then followed me back into the center lane. That was the only confirmation I needed so I did the only thing I could, punched the gas like my little Subaru had the same zip as a gas-guzzling Lamborghini. My car wasn't pretty, but it was sporty and reliable, which meant I had a good chance of getting away from the creep following me.

At least that was what I kept telling myself as I pressed down as hard as I could on the gas, trying like hell to put some distance between my car and the biker.

CREATIVELY CRUSHED

But I couldn't go home with some crazed biker on my trail, which meant my shop was off limits as well. Which wasn't helpful at all since I couldn't drive around all night. I needed reinforcements so I picked up my phone. "Hey, Jana, I need your help."

"Hey, Moon, hang on a second." Music played in the background along with the sounds of conversation and I wondered if I was interrupting a party. "Sorry about that. What can I help with?"

"Don't freak out but there's a biker following me, has been since I left the doctor's office and I don't know where to go."

"Can you just pull over somewhere that's busy and lit up?"

I shook my head and glanced in the mirror again just to make sure the biker was still following us.

"Hello, Moon? Answer me!"

"Sorry. No, there's nowhere like that until we're closer to home. Plus Beau is sleeping after another attack."

"Oh no," Jana moaned. "I'm sorry to hear that. Is he doing okay?"

"Mostly. We just left the doctor. Let's just hope this treatment works. Any ideas on how to shake this guy?"

"Come to the clubhouse. Cross has been out for hours looking for you, anyway."

Why would Cross be looking for me? We didn't have plans to meet up today and he had far more important things on his mind. "No thanks, I don't want to impose. I'll go to the police station, which should have been my first thought." Except I was a naturally suspicious person and so far Mayhem's finest left much to be desired.

"Moon, don't. Please. Just trust me and come here to the clubhouse. Please?"

There was a worry in her voice I couldn't understand but I respected it enough to at least consider it. "I'll let you know, Jana. Right now I need to think. Later."

CREATIVELY CRUSHED

Tossing the phone onto the passenger seat, I slowed to take the exit, groaning when a line of traffic ended not fifty feet after the exit ramp began.

Gridlock was the last thing I needed with an unknown biker behind me, but I kept my eye on him like there was anything I could do if he decided to come after me here in traffic. Still, I was prepared. Ready for a fight when I saw him split the lane, I rolled down the window and waited.

"What?" I growled when he cruised up to me. "What is it that you want that you followed me all this way?"

He scowled and flipped up his motorcycle mask revealing big blue eyes. Make that angry blue eyes.

"You can tell your fucking friend, White Boy—"

"That dirtbag is no friend of mine and if that's why you've been following me, you're wasting your time!" Hitting the button to slide the window closed, the biker's hand reached out to stop the window's progress.

"Go away."

"I saw him in your shop."

How was this my life right now? "Then I guess you didn't see long enough for the cops to haul him away for threatening me, after his biker buddy shot up my store!"

His eyes widened at my outburst. "Shit! Are you serious right now, because if you're lying to me lady, I swear I will make you fucking regret it."

"Believe me when I tell you that lying to another biker isn't on my schedule today. Craig is not a friend of mine, I can assure you of that, so if that's why you're following me, stop."

"I wish I could, lady, but I need answers. About my sister."

I felt bad for him, or more likely his sister, but it really wasn't my concern. Was it? "I don't have any answers and I don't know your sister."

"Why did Roadkill MC shoot up your store?"

"Isn't that the million-dollar question? Probably because a friend of mine is married to someone in another...uhm...club." I hoped I sounded more confident than the last two words because my confidence was waning.

Recognition flashed in his eyes and I hoped this man didn't represent another threat to Cross and the club. Then my father's words came back to me, something that hadn't happened in more than a decade.

The enemy of my enemy is my friend.

Chapter Twenty-Three

Cross

What the fuck?

I'd left the clubhouse and headed straight to Moon's house even though Max and Golden Boy, plus their wives, had assured me that she wasn't at home. She wasn't but maybe she had been. Sometime between Max leaving and my arrival, someone had been here. I found the door kicked open. And more, they were looking for something.

Moon's house was never disorganized. Sure there were always signs of life such as Beau's backpack hanging on the back of a dining chair they never used or one of Moon's many colorful scarves draped over whatever piece of furniture was nearest. Now her place was a fucking mess. Ransacked was the only word to describe it. Desk drawers were pulled out and papers were dumped everywhere. The brightly colored loveseat had slashes on each cushion, a clear sign that someone was looking for something. Guilt bubbled in my gut at what this mess could possibly mean.

It had to be Roadkill. I didn't know how or why, but somehow, they found out about me and Moon. It was the only thing that made sense and it fucking pissed me off. If they had her and Beau, fuck me. If they harmed one hair on their head, I'd make sure none of them lived to regret it. I tried to call Moon for the fourth or fifth time and again it went straight to voicemail.

Goddammit.

Dropping down on the sofa with my head in my hands, I let the feeling of failure settle over me. Again. It was a sick feeling of déjà vu, me leaving my woman to an unknown danger while I handled shit for the Reckless Bastards. Not that I regretted the club, because I didn't. I'd taken on being President, and I'd carried out that role to the best of my ability. It was my job, my responsibility to keep my club members and their families safe.

CREATIVELY CRUSHED

And now it looked like Moon was paying the price for it. Maybe even Beau, too. That thought make me sick to my stomach and I knew I had to get the fuck out of there and find them.

Closing the door behind me, I practically ran from Moon's house and jumped on my bike, racing through every fucking street in Mayhem in search of Moon's sporty green Subaru. It was nowhere to be found and that only compounded my anger. And my guilt. If I hadn't been trying to put some distance between us, she would have known she needed to be more careful.

Dammit! Fuck!

Moon was strong-willed and independent, used to dominating her whole world without any input from anyone else. She was one of the strongest women I'd ever met, hell that I'd ever known and now I might have lost her. Her car wasn't in Mayhem and two hours later I had confirmation she wasn't in Vegas either, at least her car wasn't. "Fuuuuuck!"

The phone rang and I tapped the Bluetooth inside my helmet. "Yeah?"

"Cross it's Jana. Moon just called and said some biker is chasing her. She doesn't want to go home and she refuses to come here."

"What? Why?" I knew it was a dick move to pull back without any explanation, but would she rather be in danger than accept my help? That was bullshit.

"Because," Jana sighed. "She said you have enough to deal with right now."

Aw, fuck. "Shit. I'm on my way back to the clubhouse. See if you can get her on the phone for me. And Jana?"

"Yeah?"

"Thank you for letting me know."

"Of course. I know Max would want to know if it was me." Her words were cryptic but with her voice bouncing around inside my helmet I could hear the smile in her words.

"He damn well better since you're his wife and the mother of his kids." While Moon and I were just having

CREATIVELY CRUSHED

fun. A lot of fun in the sack and if I was being honest, outside of it too.

I continued, "Moon is a really nice woman with a cute kid and I hate that she's mixed up in this shit because of us."

"Okaaay. If that's the lie you're still telling yourself, sure Cross." Without waiting for me to respond, which likely would have been with a few choice swear words, Jana ended the call and as soon as I could I turned my bike around, hit the throttle and headed back to the clubhouse. Feeling like an impotent fuck because I couldn't help Moon.

Jana didn't know what she was talking about. Moon wasn't serious about me, she couldn't be. She had a kid to look after and didn't need this kind of drama in her life. There may have been a time or two when I looked at her and saw more, but that was my own fucking selfishness. I wanted Moon and the more time I spent with her, the more I wanted her. Wanted to do more than fuck her. Hell, I even enjoyed those weird breathing exercises, if for no other reason than we got to sit close and her sexy, earthy scent managed to dig deep into my brain and take up residence.

Thinking about the woman had conjured her up, or maybe Jana had told her to call me because there she was on my phone.

"Hey Moon, where are you?"

"Uhm, I'm at home," she said hesitantly.

"Shit. I wish you would have answered your phone. I saw your house. I'll have some guys take care of it but not tonight. Are you okay?"

"I'm not really sure, Cross. But I need you to come to my house. Please?"

"Is everything all right?" I asked, taking a left at the next light that would take me right back to Moon. Whatever she needed, I'd be there. "Is Beau okay?"

"Cross, I'll tell you everything when you get here. Drive safely and stay calm."

I couldn't help but smile at her maternal tone. No matter how shaken she was by the mess in her house and whoever had been fucking following her, she was always the boss of her world.

And that fucking turned me on more than anything.

"See you soon." The call ended before I could ask her about who was following her and I went as fast as I could until I pulled up to her house, noting all the lights were on. The door was closed as much as it could be considering it had been kicked in. I reached behind me, pulled my piece from my waistband. and pushed the door open.

"Moon?" I called out, gun at the ready.

"In here," she called, her voice calm but there was a tremor of unease that had me moving deeper into the house. The first fucking thing I saw was some blond asshole picking up trash and shoving it into a big black trash bag. I curled my finger around the trigger. This wasn't going to end well.

"Who the fuck are you?" My eyes darted around the room until I saw Moon safe and unharmed. "What's going on?"

"Calm, remember? And put that thing away in my house."

I wanted to shake the woman. How in the hell was I supposed to remain calm with some strange asshole in her house?

"I am calm," I told her and spotted a black leather *kutte* draped over the arm of the big sofa. I lowered my piece but kept it in my hand. "Now help me stay calm by telling my why you have one of the Sons of Sin inside your house."

She sighed and stepped between us, one hand on my chest to keep me from killing the mother fucker. "Cross, calm. Beau had a bad attack and he's upstairs sleeping."

"Another attack?" I slid my piece back into the waistband of my jeans. If she was calm after all this, I'd be calm as well. "Shit, how is he doing? What did the doctor say?"

Her smile was warm and affectionate, so was the caress of her hand from my chest down to my belt. "Later. This is Cordell, I mean Ripcord. Sorry," she flashed the man an apologetic grin.

"Yeah, I saw the *kutte*. Was he the asshole chasing you?"

She nodded but Ripcord spoke up. "I was and it was a misunderstanding."

"Then make me understand it." I knew I was coming across as an asshole, but I didn't give a shit, not now. I would break this mother fucker in two if he'd hurt Moon.

"Boys. Settle down. I have a sleeping son upstairs, so use your inside voices and have a seat." Moon motioned to the dining room table and smiled at Ripcord. "Thank you for helping clean up the mess."

I snorted at her sincere gratitude. "Are you that sure he wasn't the cause of it? Because a lot of this shit doesn't add up."

Ripcord sighed. "I did do it, which is why I helped clean up this mess. And Moon has already accepted my apology," he said defiantly. "I was looking for information on my little sister."

"Why in the fuck would—" Moon's hand on my shoulder stopped my tirade cold. She smiled at me and honestly, what the fuck could I do but shut the fuck up and stare at that beautiful smile. Even slightly tousled and rumpled in her yellow outfit that showed off her shoulders and a beautiful hummingbird tattoo, she was a vision.

"After talking with Cordell," she said and took a seat beside me and dropped a hand on top of mine, "some things have become clear, mainly that you two have a common enemy."

I glanced at Ripcord and this time without judgment, I could see concern and fear written all over his face. Still, I didn't know too many of the Sons of Sin members personally, since most of them were from up North, so I would reserve judgment until I did. "Yeah, who?"

"Who else?" she asked with a roll of her eyes. "Roadkill." Her gaze seared through me, begging me to stay calm and listen. When I nodded my agreement, she stood and went to the head of the table staring at each of us. "Cordell has a sister and she's been missing for almost a full year, Cross. She's fifteen."

"Fuck." I stared at Ripcord who looked ready to rip someone's head off.

"Yeah," Moon sighed and sent a sympathetic look to the angry man across from me. "Cordell spotted her on a website for those in search of companionship from girls of a certain age. The website is run by Roadkill and Cordell thought, mistakenly, that Craig was a friend of mine because he saw him in my shop."

Ripcord nodded. "And I ransacked her place thinking I could find evidence of this underage bullshit. That's not some shit they'd keep at the clubhouse."

I snorted. "Not that you have a chance in hell of getting inside the Roadkill clubhouse."

"Not yet, anyway. I'm working on it." He turned to Moon. "I really am sorry about messing up your shit, but I was desperate."

She waved him off. "You can replace the furniture but right now we need to focus. You both have a common enemy. Maybe a little teamwork is in order?"

I let my shoulders fall in resignation. I didn't love the idea of bringing more people into the storm that was my life right now but I appreciated—more than she could know—that she thought of me when she heard his story. "Shit."

"Yeah. What problems are you having with Roadkill?" Ripcord looked at me intently, waiting for me to spill my secrets.

I looked at Moon, who shrugged. "This is your story to tell, not mine."

"So fucking reasonable," I grumbled while she laughed easily. With great reluctance, I filled him in on some of the problems with Roadkill and the whole goddamn city. "It's always something these days with the city, trying to shut down our businesses. And Roadkill, they're just a fucking pain."

I told him all about Vigo working with the feds because any MC worth their fucking salt would have rules against snitching. His eyes went wide when I mentioned the political corruption.

"Damn, man. Where's Vigo now?"

"Dead." That was all he needed to know.

"Good." Ripcord gave a short nod of respect, which I returned. I couldn't blame a man for doing what he had to do to find his kid sister, especially if his story was true.

"Better than good," Moon said with a loud clap. "I'm happy to have facilitated this meeting but I need you to go so I can scrub this place and keep an eye on my son."

Both of us stood, feeling bad to have kept her occupied when she clearly had other shit on her mind.

"I'll take these to the cans." Ripcord held four bags with an expectant look on his face.

"Side of the house," I said at the same time Moon did. I turned to Moon with a look of my own. "Busy day?"

She grinned. "You could say that."

I wanted to ask more but Ripcord's boots were loud as fuck on the steps and I pulled back. Moon stepped around me so she stood between us, always the damn peacemaker.

"Sorry to scare you. I appreciate you trying to help, for real." I reached for my piece when he dug into his pocket but it was just a wad of cash. Ripcord pulled off a few bills, at least three grand from what I could tell. "For furniture and cleaning," he grinned and waved before heading back toward the door.

"Good luck finding your sister, Cordell."

He froze and sent her a sad smile. "Yeah, thanks."

"You have somewhere I can get in touch with you?" I still didn't know if this guy and his MC were full of shit but Moon was right. If Roadkill was their enemy, we had common ground.

"Yeah. SoS Auto Restoration." With a final nod, he was gone.

Moon sighed as she turned to me and wrapped her arms around my waist. "Sorry to worry you."

"I'm sorry Beau had another attack." I let my arms wrap around her body, rubbing one hand up and down her back before dropping a kiss on top of her head. "How are you holding up?"

She sighed and leaned further into me with a moan. "Better now that he is, but still shaken."

"Sorry to add to it sweetheart, but we're on lockdown which means that you and little man are coming with me. No arguments." I inhaled her deep floral scent, closing my eyes and counted down the seconds until she pulled away and rattled off a dozen reasons why she couldn't—or wouldn't—come with me.

She did pull back and tired light green eyes looked up into mine, searching for an answer I was pretty sure

I didn't have. "Okay. Do you think you can put some shoes on Beau while I pack an overnight bag?"

I nodded, relieved and worried by how easily she agreed. But I'd deal with that once I was sure they were safe. "No problem, but you might want to make it a few nights."

She froze but nodded, deciding once again not to argue. "How bad is it?"

"Pretty fucking bad. We just found out some shit and once it gets out, no one who means anything to us will be safe." We both silently chose to ignore the importance of that comment. For now.

"What's wrong, Cross?"

I cupped her face and looked deep into her eyes, so light green they were almost eerie. "I thought I failed you too when I stood in here earlier."

Moon's soft hands went to my face, tilting me down until I looked her right in those bossy green eyes. "You didn't fail anyone. Don't even think that, Cross, especially not now. You need all the confidence you can muster for this fight and I can't be the only one of us who believes in you. But," she raised up on her toes and pressed soft pink lips against mine. It was soft and too damn short. "If you want, when this is all over, I'll tell you what a dick you were. Okay?"

A laugh bubbled out of me but I couldn't respond because her belief in me was humbling. Empowering. This time I held Moon close and kissed her for so long I lost track of time and place, and what we both should've been doing. The taste of her, the scent of her and the way she submitted to my kiss, had me drunk with power.

Eventually I pulled back with a reluctant grin. "I'm holding you to that." After another kiss that was too damn short, we both sprang into action.

Chapter Twenty-Four

Moon

"Why are we staying here Mom? Is something wrong with our house?" Thankfully Beau had fallen asleep about a mile away from Dr. Mankowski's office and hadn't seen the damage to our home. After that, he'd slept soundly in Cross's arms when we left for the clubhouse. And since the parenting gods had been shining down on me, he'd waited two whole days to ask the obvious question.

I didn't have a good answer, at least not one that satisfied me as I looked around the barren room that had no personal touches. But Cross seemed legitimately worried about our safety, and I took that very seriously.

"Not exactly, no."

He frowned and stopped his careful browsing, turning towards me.

"Are bad men after us?"

I pulled my boy closer and hugged him tight, letting him know that he was loved and safe. "Sometimes when adults want to hurt each other, they go after people who are close to them, like friends and family."

"Why?"

He was so inquisitive it always amazed me. "Well I imagine they think it will hurt more." I shouldn't even be having this conversation with someone Beau's age but the more he understood about what was happening, the calmer he would be later.

"Don't worry, Mom. Cross will keep us safe." Beau was so full of confidence in a man he didn't know that well that I almost believed him. I hoped Cross could keep us safe and I believed he would. But there was a niggling doubt, and I'd feel a lot better if I knew who the big bad was. "We should decorate this room for Cross!"

CREATIVELY CRUSHED

Once again he was right. Looking around Cross's room, it was bare, not one photo in sight. Not even of his wife. His parents. Other than deodorant and cologne and a few outfits that hung in the closet, the room was austere and all but empty. Beau and I had brought more stuff than was already in here.

"That's a good idea but let's not go crazy, maybe start with a couple drawings."

"Okay. Jana has art supplies in front, can I go draw with her?" I gave a quick nod and his feet took off. He yanked the door open and ran smack into his second favorite person in the world.

"Hi Cross! I'm going to make some drawings for your room. Bye!"

Cross chuckled at his energy, stepping inside the room and filling it instantly. "To have that kind of energy right now."

"Or anytime," I agreed with a smile. And then something stopped me in my tracks. Beau's energy level. He'd been running around these last few days like a normal kid. No wheezing. No coughing. Could it be true? The stem cell treatments had started to work? A brush of hopefulness and gratitude rushed through me but before I could indulge it, Cross was asking for my attention.

"Are you guys okay here?" he asked.

"Yeah. Better safe than sorry regardless if we want to be here, or if we're important to the club, right?" The words came out harsher than I expected, and it was stupid to wish for a different answer, but for now, I decided I wouldn't deny my feelings for him, at least not to myself.

He opened his mouth to say something and then closed it. For a second, I thought I saw disappointment flash across his handsome face, but then I remembered, he was still in love with someone else.

"I know none of this is personal, Cross, we'll be fine."

"Thanks for that thing with Ripcord," he said. "It was stupid as hell but also brave and very helpful."

CREATIVELY CRUSHED

Brave and helpful? Just what every woman wanted to hear, right? I crossed my arms and stared at him for a long time, wishing I'd never gotten involved with him while mentally calculating what I could do to have more time with him. "Thank you, I guess."

His mouth curled into a sensual smile. "Think we have time for a proper thanks?"

I most certainly did. "If I say no, will you take it as a challenge?"

"Damn fucking right, I will." Cross's booted foot kicked the door shut and he twisted the lock before advancing on me and pressing his body against mine. He pushed me down on the bed. "It's been too fucking long, Moon. I need you."

His voice was low and dark, raw with need as he stripped me out of my clothes and tore off my panties.

"Cross, don't tease."

But he did, lightly brushing his fingers up and down my pussy lips, drawing a shiver out.

"But teasing you is so fun, Moon." He applied more pressure, little by little, until I was crazed with need. Then he slipped a thick finger inside me and I arched my back and closed my eyes.

"Yes."

"Fuck, I love how hungry you are for me." His finger twisted and I moved closer, crying out my pleasure. "Yes."

Cross groaned and pulled me closer, grabbing me by the waist and flipping me over on my knees. He lifted me up until I rested on all fours.

"Now that you have me here, what will you do with me?" Just the sight of him over my shoulder had me aching with desire.

"You want me to tell you how I'm going to slide my tongue inside your asshole, finger fucking you until you beg me to make you come?"

I nodded, feeling breathless as more desire leaked out of me.

"Or do you want me to tell you how much you'll love it when I eat your pussy and finger your ass, making you come so hard your juices run all over me. Then I'm going to drink every last drop before I fuck you until you pass out."

"I...I'm liking the sound of that." I liked it too much but my body didn't care. His words were like dousing a fire with kerosene and the only thing I wanted was for his words to become reality. "What are you waiting for?"

"Until you're ready, Moon."

"I'm ready," I insisted.

He shook his head with a smile, looking like the bad boy next door with his dark hair and tattoos that gave him a devil-may-care air that only added to his appeal. And he had my mouth watering as he undressed. "Not yet, you're not. Turn around."

I did as he commanded. That deep voice so smooth and thick like honey sent a shiver straight through me. And Cross knew what he was doing, the waiting. The anticipating. It built up my expectation, it tortured me. It thrilled me.

And when his tongue finally touched me, exactly where and how he promised, I did beg him. I begged for more of his wicked tongue, more of everything. "Please," I begged, desperate for release.

My legs collapsed when he gave me what I begged for, the pulsing vibrations of his laugh had another orgasm building quickly within me.

"Keep going. Let go, baby, he ordered as he turned me over and put his mouth on me, fulfilling every dirty word until another orgasm rushed out of me in just seconds.

"Cross," I cried out his name when he turned me back over on my knees and slid into me from behind, his warm breath fanning down my back. His breath came out in short shallow bursts as aftershocks pulsed around him.

"Moon, fuck. Yes." His words were raw and gritty, hitting me right where I needed them.

"Oh, fuck." The pleasure in his voice sent warmth rushing through me, down to my cunt and soaking us where we were joined.

"Fuck!"

"Cross." His strokes were long and deep, slow. Sensual and all-consuming. I nearly fell right then and there.

Over the edge.

Into love.

Maybe.

One hand went to my breast, kneading and squeezing as he thrust into me. Long, deep strokes that shook the bed and touched me to my soul.

"You're mine, baby." He repeated the words over and over again like it was a spell he'd conjured up. Over and over as he pushed me closer and closer to the edge of everything. And when his teeth sank into the soft skin between my neck and shoulder, I fell.

Completely.

One tear slipped from the corner of my eye and I was happy I was face down on the bed, so he couldn't see me. When a pounding knock rattled the door, I felt nothing but relief.

However temporary it turned out to be.

Chapter Twenty-Five

Cross

"The bottom line is, we have no beef with the Reckless Bastards and Ripcord thinks we might be able to help each other out."

The Sons of Sin MC President, Gage, looked at me with a serious expression on his face. There was no bullshit posturing or anything. They knew this was serious shit, just as we did.

"I think so, too," I admitted reluctantly. It wasn't just Moon's advice or gentle push, it was the right decision for the club. And having another MC's help would increase our chances of getting out of this shit alive.

"We have a lot of balls in the air right now, but you let me know if you find anything out and I'll do the same."

Gage nodded, easily accepting the answer. "You really think you can take down a politician?"

I grinned. "Haven't you been watching the news, Gage?"

"No shit?" He shot back, voice filled with awe. "In that case, I hope to talk to you soon, Cross."

I nodded at Gage and hopped back on my bike, eager to get back to the clubhouse. And if I was being honest, Moon too. The past week had been too hectic and we hadn't spent as much time together as I would have liked and the fact that I wanted to spend more time with her meant I might have to start living my life again.

But I couldn't dwell on it, not until this Roadkill and Pacheco bullshit was behind us. When I arrived at the clubhouse I had one thing on my mind, a sweet taste of Moon's addictive mouth but it wasn't her pretty face I saw when I walked in.

"Hey man, I got something to show you. Two things actually." Jag met me at the door, walking beside me. "The Sun just ran a front page story outlining the corruption of Pacheco and they claim to have proof that he's a stakeholder in the sale of underage girls."

The shit-eating grin he wore was a goddamn welcome sight to see.

"Thank fuck some media outlets are still interested in the fucking news, right?" I took the paper from him, listening with half an ear while skimming the article. In just the course of a week they'd managed to find the one thing we couldn't.

"Damn, they took what you sent and turned it into dynamite. Fucking dynamite, man."

Jag dropped down at one of the tables and grinned. "They found what we couldn't and I'm damn glad they did. Pacheco's gotta be shittin' in his pants right now."

I hoped that fucker was scared shitless. "Everyone else see this?"

Gunnar and Savior nodded, Lasso shrugged and the rest gave halfhearted nods because as good as it was, it would be better if that fucker didn't take another breath.

Ever.

"If he isn't yet, he will be soon. I also got something from Vivi." Jag turned the screen to me and I frowned.

"Uh, man I'm glad you got photos from your girl, but this isn't the kind of shit you share."

Gunnar let out a loud guffaw. "Dude we're happy you're getting phone sex or cybersex or whatever, but that ain't exactly club business."

Jag frowned and turned the image back around. It wasn't all that bad, just plenty of cleavage, more than he probably wanted us to see. "It's got encrypted data in it you dumb fuck. Not even her tits if you must know. You fuckers are sick."

Gunnar let out another thunderous laugh at being able to get a rise out of calm and cool Jag. "Then turn it back around and let me look at it."

CREATIVELY CRUSHED

"Dick," Jag muttered again before turning the screen back my way. "This just came in with all the shit the Sun uncovered, but we also got the website data. I was able to ID a few of the girls and though I can't confirm it, I think this is Ripcord's sister. Jessica Stephens."

Shit. She had the same blonde hair and same blue eyes as her brother. "Do we have an address or anything?"

"I'm working on it."

"Good."

I could deal with a lot when it came to ways to make money that weren't strictly on the up and up, but teenage pussy was off limits and for that sin alone, I'd kill every single one of those motherfuckers.

"Holy shit. You gotta see this, Cross."

I looked up at the screen that faced me again and whistled. "No fucking way?"

"What? Let me see," Gunnar insisted like a school girl eager for gossip. "Holy fucking shit, is this for real?"

"Vivi wouldn't send it if it wasn't."

And what she had sent was the fucking nail in Pacheco's coffin.

"What do you want to do with this?" Jag asked.

The answer was simple. "I want this shit to lead the news for the rest of the goddamn week," I said.

But first I needed to give Ripcord a head's up. "Give me thirty minutes and then send it out with the missing person's report for Jessica."

Fuck me, I didn't want to have to be the one to deliver this kind of news. Because I had so much shit to deal with, I called up Gage. It was his club, his man. He could deal with that shit.

"I'll be back."

"Be happy, Prez! We got those fuckers now!" Gunnar pounded his fist on the table and howled like a goddamn loon.

I was happy but the closer we got to Pacheco's bullshit, the bigger the target was on our backs.

Chapter Twenty-Six

Moon

The past few days had been tense and everyone was starting to feel stir crazy from being cooped up in the Reckless Bastards compound all week. Their hospitality was nice and I felt safe enough to stay, but cabin fever was starting to set in. I joined Jana, Teddy, Rocky and Mandy at a picnic table behind the clubhouse filled with food and lemonade. It was nice, feeling like I had a group of friends to sit around and just talk with, and pretend like there wasn't danger lurking around every corner.

"But what I really wanna know," Jana began with a mischievous smile and a soft caress of her belly, "is what's going on with you and Cross, Moon?"

I blinked at the sound of my name and looked up at four pairs of expectant eyeballs. "We're enjoying each other's company, that's all." I didn't bother to tell them I wanted more because I knew Cross didn't have anything to give to anyone other than Lauren.

And I wouldn't take that from him—or her.

Teddy arched a perfectly sculpted auburn brow and leaned back in her seat. "Because of the whole biker thing? Because I had that same thought when Jana first met Max, but these guys are bigger marshmallows than the guys I worked with when I was a model. And Cross is fuckin' hot. Not as hot as my Tate but hot, nevertheless."

"No, not because of the biker thing, Teddy." Not that I could reasonably say anything else while surrounded by four women married to or engaged to be married to a family of bikers.

"Then, what?" Teddy's expression was pure disbelief but it didn't bother me.

"It's the whole still in love with his wife thing." I stared right back at Teddy, daring her to give me a hard time, but she didn't. Instead her expression softened, and she did that sympathetic head tilt that could produce rage in me like no other, so I looked away.

Jana's big green eyes blinked slowly, shocked. "I'm surprised he even told you about her. He never talks about her."

Probably because he didn't want to share her with anyone. I shrugged off her effort to make the secret into something it wasn't. "People always tell me things they shouldn't or don't want to. It's a gift, or a curse, I suppose." Though that one time a woman confessed that she was cheating on her husband with his sister had left even me shocked.

"You're wrong, and scared," Jana accused, her steely glare daring me to challenge her. "That's okay, we were all scared once."

I shook my head, refusing to let her words or their determined and eager head nods sway me. I knew the truth. "I can't put myself in a situation that I know will end badly, especially with everything I have on my plate. I need to make good choices for me and Beau."

Teddy and Rocky both laughed. "I find good choices to be terribly boring," the stunning redhead said with a laugh.

"Maybe but I'm all Beau has and I can't afford to lose my shit over a man, especially one who has heartache written all over him. Boring is preferable to broken."

"Who said anything about broken?" Rocky asked, far too astutely. "Oh shit, you like him. Like seriously maybe-could be love, kind of like?"

I shook my head silently.

"That's bullshit Moon and you know it," Jana said with more ferocity than I expected. "It's not just you and Beau anymore. You have us. All of us."

I accepted their kind words because it was the only thing to do in the moment. Cross was their family, technically the boss of their men and I knew how break ups in a situation like this worked. I'd seen it plenty with my family's social circle. Usually the couples all kept the half of the couple with the most power or influence, so usually the husband. I vowed that after this was all over, I'd do better about getting out and making new friends.

Living life.

"Thanks, ladies." My phone vibrated in my pocket and I pulled it out, frowning at the unknown number. "Excuse me. Hello?" I got up from the table and walked to a spot where I could hear.

"Is this Moonbeam Vanderbilt?"

I didn't recognize the almost robotic voice but immediately I went on alert. "Who's asking?"

"Please confirm your identity, ma'am." The voice on the other end spoke with an air of authority and a whole lot of irritation.

"You first."

"Officer Jones," he grunted out angrily.

"That's a common name, do you have a first name?" What kind of cop called without identifying themselves?

"No."

"Okay, neither do I. Have a good day." I ended the call and took a quick glance over my shoulder where Beau played with the other kids but mostly he climbed up Stitch's long body which was perfect since he was little more than a kid himself. My phone rang again and I went in search of Jag. I couldn't be sure, but if the caller was a cop, he was a crooked one.

Jag looked up when I placed a hand on his shoulder and I pointed at the ringing phone. "What's up?"

I answered the phone on speaker. "Hello?"

"Ms. Vanderbilt?"

"Who's calling?" I couldn't help but smile at the frustrated growl he let out.

"Officer Jones." Jag grabbed the phone from my hands and did a bunch of quick hand moves before he handed it back. The call was recording and I relaxed.

CREATIVELY CRUSHED

"Officer Jones who refuses to identify himself properly? Tell you what, keep your first name and give me your badge number."

"Are you Moonbeam Vanderbilt, mother of Rainbeau Vanderbilt?"

"How is this any of your business? I don't even know who you are."

"There's been an accident at the camp, Ms. Vanderbilt."

Jag's dark brows rose in question and I shook my head, pointing at the area just outside where Beau played with his friends.

"And what does that have to do with me?"

The faux officer sighed heavily. "We think one of the injured kids is your son, Rainbeau. That is your son's name, isn't it?"

"You think? Well when you have your facts straight Officer Jones, let me know. It's pretty reckless to pass out this information if you don't have any real answers."

"You're saying Rainbeau isn't yours? Little kid with black hair?"

"Nope, I'm saying it's none of your business. Officer." It probably wasn't smart to taunt a police officer or a gangster, but when he messed with my kid, he would get a fight right back.

"Yeah, you think you're so smart, you dirty bitch! Wouldn't it be a shame if something happened to that little bastard?" After that he hung up the phone and Jag took the phone from me.

"That was rough but don't worry, Moon. We'll get that asshole."

He walked away with my phone and I walked to the window, staring at my boy who was having a ball using Stitch as a Jungle Jim.

"I hope so."

In fact, I hoped they found the caller and systematically dismantled everything that mattered to him, and that vengeful thought only made me angry.

CREATIVELY CRUSHED

"Hey, you look like you're ready to slug someone." Cross's hands landed on my shoulders in a soothing caress. "Everything okay?"

I shook my head and told him about the phone call. "Pretty sure he just threatened me, but I will be fine."

"He did," Jag said when he returned and handed over my phone. "It was smart to hang up and force him to call back. It's taken care of, or at least it will be soon. Very soon."

"So we're still on lockdown?" I looked up at Cross for an answer and he nodded with a sympathetic smile.

"Yep. Sorry babe."

"You don't look even a little bit sorry."

His grin widened. "I'm not."

Truth was, I wasn't sorry either. Spending this time with Cross was nice even though the circumstances weren't ideal. I knew I'd be disappointed when it came to an end.

But for now, I'd enjoy every minute I had with him.

Chapter Twenty-Seven

Cross

The clubhouse was tense all week. We were all on edge because of the wall to wall news coverage about the biggest political scandal to hit Nevada since the mob took over Vegas. All the news anchors couldn't help but talk about the evidence linking Bill Pacheco and a few other government officials to a website that sold underage girls. Kids. Fucking little girls like Ripcord's kid sister.

It was good that it was all anyone was talking about; that could only be good news for us. But it also meant Roadkill was more determined than ever to retaliate since they were about to lose their cash cow and maybe their freedom.

The proof was in their petty retaliation, vandalizing one of our dispensaries a few days ago. The damage was minimal, mostly they broke a lot of bongs and glass pipes, the glass doors on the fridges and the display cases. But the dumbasses had given themselves up by not stealing the cash or the weed. They were planning something.

"Sons of Sin are here," Lasso said, and everyone stood collectively.

We'd been planning for the past few days and today was the day it would all come to a fucking head.

"Five minutes and then we head out!" I wound my way through the clubhouse to the back bedrooms because, for once, I was doing exactly what all of my men were. I found Moon and laid a kiss on her that would sustain me through this shit show until I could sink into her slick pussy once again.

We rode out to the south side of the property with the Sons of Sin MC to plot out how tonight would go. Me, Savior and Stitch left the group to start phase one of our plan, which began at the Roadkill MC compound. We tiptoed onto the property as soon as the sun went down and the dumbasses made our job easy

CREATIVELY CRUSHED

because all the bikes, cars and ATV's were parked in one spot.

"Too bad we can't just blow these fuckers up." Savior was a crazy motherfucker who worked hard all night to get the explosives ready for tonight.

"That wouldn't help our plan, would it?" As much as it would solve all of our problems to just put these explosives all around their main clubhouse, I wanted them to suffer. A lot.

"Okay," Stitch strolled up with his confident gait and a satisfied smile on his face. "My bag is empty."

"Mine too," I said with a grin. "It's a good thing these cocky fuckers are too stupid to do perimeter sweeps while they party. Must be nice not to have worries."

Forty minutes later we crept off the property and went back to the meeting spot.

"All done?" Gunnar clapped his hands, eager to get on with kicking some ass.

"Yep. In twenty minutes, we'll get in position and in thirty we'll set off the alarms at the dispensary," I answered.

Ripcord nodded but I could see his nerves, which reminded me of myself about a decade and a half ago when I was still earning my bones as a young Bastard. "What if they don't come?"

"They will," I assured him. "They've been planning this at least since the night of the break-in, and it would be better for them if we all ended up dead. That was their plan and our plan is to fuck up theirs, by striking first."

Ripcord nodded and slid a glance to his President. Gage didn't look happy about any of it but he knew like I did that if we didn't act first, Roadkill would not stop. A look passed between the two men. Resolve and resignation. Tonight might not be pretty but it was fucking necessary.

When the alarm sounded inside the dispensary we were all on alert. Jag was back at the clubhouse keeping an eye on the women and children as well as

CREATIVELY CRUSHED

us. We had wireless comms so he could direct us when the shit turned chaotic. Lasso, Golden Boy, Stitch and Savior were inside with two Sons of Sin. The rest of us were on our bikes about a quarter-mile away, ready to strike as soon as Roadkill crossed our paths.

The energy crackled in the air like one of those nights where a desert storm struck out of nowhere. The hair stood up on the back of my neck, down my arms and all over my body. It was the same feeling I'd had in combat, when the enemy was close, and I knew there was about to be a fight to the death. That was what tonight was; not everyone would survive.

This was war.

The sound of motorcycles in the distance had everyone falling quiet. Still, like an immovable river. About sixty seconds after the last bike raced past us, we rode in two straight lines the whole way there. Silent. Focused.

Deadly focused.

The dumbasses parked right up front, not at all suspicious. We moved quiet and perfectly in sync, even the Sons of Sin, into the dispensary. White Boy Craig stood at the center of nearly a dozen men, armed but not protected.

"Come on out boys, you're outnumbered," he laughed, completely oblivious to his own fucking danger. "We counted four bikes out front so unless some of you are sittin' bitch, we got you."

They tossed out a few high-fives and talked some shit while we moved in, Ripcord with a gun aimed right at White Boy Craig's back.

"You always were a dumb fuck, White Boy. I guess that's why you can't count." Before he could even turn around, Ripcord squeezed off two shots. One in each of his knees.

Craig went down, crying like a little bitch. "My fucking knees! You shot me in the fucking knees!"

"You're lucky it wasn't your fucking dick, asshole."

CREATIVELY CRUSHED

Those were the last words I could hear because bullets started flying and they were coming from all directions. Ripcord had White Boy Craig more than handled so I got to work helping take down the other pieces of shit. In the distance I heard the explosives going off like it was the Fourth of July and New Years Eve combined, telling me that the Roadkill who'd been on stakeout bought it good.

Lu had a bullet in his gut and writhed on the ground in pain while I caught two prospects running like hell towards the exit.

Cowards. That's what happened when a fucked up MC recruited the most fucked up minds they could find and turned them even crazier. It couldn't have been more than two or three minutes when the dispensary fell silent.

Mostly.

"You fuckers set us up!"

"Quit your fuckin' bitchin'."

"You won't get away with this. The cops will be here and there's no way you can cover this shit up." Craig looked so pleased with himself.

"There you go, trying to think for yourself again. I got three words for you dumb shit, stand your ground." Ripcord took the butt of his gun and brought it down on Craig's temple, knocking him out cold.

Jag called in. "Hey Cross, we got the coordinates on the girls."

"Dispatch the last group and tell those fuckers to be careful, these girls will be scared as shit." That was the last thing we needed.

"Uh, actually the Feds are here. Not inside the clubhouse but in Mayhem. Trafficking is the Feds' jurisdiction and as soon as the story hit, the task force landed in town. They're eager for our help but they made it clear—"

"That they run the show? Fucking dick lickers." I didn't give a damn who got them, as long as they were safe. "Fine. Send a few guys to help."

"Will do. Tanya is on her way up there and she said she didn't think she had to remind us, but keep your fucking mouths shut until she gets there."

"Thanks, man. Talk soon."

I looked around at the carnage around us and sighed heavily. It wasn't how I planned for things to go but if it hadn't been them it would have been us.

"All right boys, guns on the ground. Everyone but Stitch and Gage, get the fuck out. Fast."

The sound of sirens grew closer and closer, the signs of a long fucking night ahead.

Chapter Twenty-Eight

Moon

"Mom! Mom! There's a girl outside and she's with a police officer."

Beau was an even bigger ball of energy from being cooped up inside all day or from an overload of testosterone and before I could ask any more questions, he was through the door again.

"Beau, wait up!" Having his scheduled disrupted was making him difficult to manage and as much as I wanted more time with Cross, I could use less of the strong headed man routine from my little boy. I walked as fast as I could without running, but Jag with his eagle vision spotted me. I slowed down when he called my name.

"Everything okay?" he asked.

I shook my head because as soon as he asked the question, as soon as the words were out, I felt confirmation of my fears. "I don't think so. Beau said a girl was outside with a cop and that just doesn't make sense. Does it?"

"Fuck no. I'm coming with you." Jag walked beside me, stopping only when we reached the opaque glass doors.

"Oh, it's only Detective Haynes." He was useless but seemed harmless.

"*Only* doesn't apply when it comes to cops, Moon."

I nodded but the defense of the detective died on my lips because he was right. What was the detective doing here and why did he have that young girl with him?

"Duly noted."

"No problem. I'm right here if you need help, remember that."

CREATIVELY CRUSHED

I did, taking a deep breath and pushing the door open. My heart raced and my legs felt like limp noodles but I managed to stay upright. "Detective, what brings you by?"

"Where's your boyfriend?"

"Go inside, Beau." I stared at my defiant son until he gave up and marched away from the young girl with the dirty face.

"But, Mom—"

I shook my head. "Now, Beau."

"Okay." With all the drama of a pre-teen he dragged himself away.

When he was gone, Haynes' smile transformed from an overworked decent guy smile to evil incarnate. "Cute kid. It really would be too bad if something happened to him."

"What did you say?"

He snarled. "I said it would be too bad if something happened to him. You got hearing problems?"

"Officer Jones," I said numbly.

"Yeah, you fucked me good, bitch."

I grinned, feeling pleased with myself. "Damn. Never would have taken you for a dirty cop."

The girl winced when he squeezed her arm and finally I looked at her, little more than a child. "Are you okay, honey?"

She nodded but it was filled with fear.

"She's fine, better than you're gonna be. For now."

I didn't know what he meant but dwelling on it wouldn't help me now. "Jessica?"

Wide blue eyes snapped to mine, surprise written all over them. She gave a barely imperceptible nod and that gave me the fuel I needed to keep going.

"Don't worry about her name, just tell your boyfriend to get out here. Now!"

CREATIVELY CRUSHED

"I don't have a boyfriend, Detective. Maybe you could ask for him by name?"

"Cross. I want to speak to Cross."

I kept my voice calm and did just what Jag had instructed. "He went to one of the dispensaries tonight, something about vandalism."

"Bullshit. Get him right now or I'll put a bullet in her fucking head." Jessica shrieked so loud it echoed in the air. "Don't make me ask again."

"Ask as many times as you want. Cross isn't here. But you know that, it's why you showed up now, isn't it?"

"You don't know what the fuck you're talking about." He shook his head. "I'll never understand what the fuck women like you are thinking, getting mixed up with these guys. They're criminals, you know that."

"And what, I should hook up with a man with a badge and an itchy trigger finger? At least these guys are honest about who they are."

"A fucking gang, that's who."

I laughed at his hypocrisy. "And aren't you part of the biggest gang around? I guess it's hard to see when you're in so deep, or maybe you don't care that Pacheco is a pedophile. Either way, my guess is you're just as guilty."

"I don't fuck no kids!"

"You just help them get sold to vile men looking to do terrible things to them, right? My bad. You're a real American hero, Detective." His face was red with anger and the hand with the gun twitched. "Kidnapping is still against the law, isn't it?"

"You can't kidnap someone who doesn't exist," he said with the kind of confidence that only came from carrying a badge and a gun. The dirtier they were, the more confident they appeared.

"Yeah?" I pulled my phone from my front pocket and snapped a photo, not caring at all that he was temporarily blinded. "Let's see what the Feds think about that image." My fingers fumbled to turn the recording on, but eventually I got it.

CREATIVELY CRUSHED

"Delete that now or I'll put a bullet in you and your little fucking bastard."

"Let the girl go and I will."

Haynes shook his head. "You have no bargaining power here, Moon. I'm an officer of the law."

"Are you? Because from where I stand, you look like a criminal."

"Fuck you, now get your goddamn greasy boyfriend out here," he snarled, and I figured I'd touched a nerve. Probably the word was out he was corrupt.

"I told you, he's not here." I heard Jag rack the slide on his gun behind me which gave me a little more confidence. But I also knew he wasn't a cop killer. Bad cop or not. "My guess is that your connection with Pacheco screwed you. I mean who would ever believe a cop who likes to have sex with children?"

"You stupid fucking bitch!" The detective raised his hand in the air and squeezed the trigger. Twice. I shuddered. The *good* cop was the one who was deranged. "The next bullet goes in her head."

"If you do that, you might as well put a bullet in your own head because since you barged onto the property without an invite or a warrant, you've been recorded. Video and audio."

"It won't hold up because these assholes are gangbangers. Nothing more than common fucking criminals."

I shrugged. "Maybe so, but Jessica is a victim. Kidnapped and trafficked then further abused by a sick deranged cop. And such a pretty girl too, the press is going to love that."

"I never fucking touched those girls!" he insisted as though that made it all right.

"You're touching her right now. Manhandling her after what she's been through. Save your hero story for the jury because I'm not buying it."

Vehicles sounded in the distance and he turned, giving me the perfect opportunity to motion to Jessica.

CREATIVELY CRUSHED

"Looks like we've got company." He grinned with confidence, thinking he had the upper hand but I knew Jag would have warned the guys before they hit the curve that led to the parking lot. "And having Cross see you laid out and lifeless will be the perfect end to this."

I held my breath at his words, keeping my breathing steady and calm when he aimed his black service weapon right at my head. Nothing could calm me down in that moment. Nothing except Jessica with wide, scared eyes. "It'll be worth it, knowing you'll be treated like one of those young girls when you get to prison."

My heart raced in anticipation of what was to come, the unimaginable pain of a bullet tearing through me. The thought of never seeing or holding my little boy again and then I froze.

Why was I giving up?

"It's cute you think any of this will make it to the light of day. That's the problem with you hippies, you're so fucking naïve."

"See Detective, that's where you're wrong. I'm not fucking naïve. In fact, I'm pretty fucking awesome." My heart pounded in my ears and I had to do all I could to get this guy to talk. Stall for time. "You and your dirty cops should have done your homework, because if you had, you'd know I'm not a dirty hippie."

His eyes flashed surprise and I knew it was wrong to enjoy it so much, but I did. "My name isn't even Moon. It's Carolina Collinswood, which probably means nothing to you."

"Less than nothing," he snorted.

"Of course it wouldn't, but my father is Les Collinswood." In addition to marrying my blue blood mother, my father had served as Governor of Connecticut and currently worked for the Director of National Intelligence.

"Oh and Mom is Marseille Hampton-Collinswood." Her father had worked as the ambassador to China while her mother had been a model and then a linguist. I had what some people would call an impeccable pedigree.

CREATIVELY CRUSHED

"Bullshit."

"Believe it or not, you'll learn the truth soon enough." We didn't get along, but I knew Daddy loved me in his own overbearing way. What I also knew was that in his eyes, only family could make you feel bad about your life choices. No one else.

"I'll take my chances."

His finger curled around the trigger. One shot sounded, maybe two, I couldn't tell as I jumped out of the way. Well, I tried but it turned out bullets traveled fast. Really fast. One grazed my side as I turned away from the gun and I fell to the ground. I didn't know where the other one landed and I didn't care all that much, not with the warmth seeping from my side.

Beau. All I could think about was Beau.

"Oh, please be okay lady! Please!" Jessica's long blonde hair hung over me like a curtain, shielding my view which made me panic.

"Jessica, get down!" I pulled her down and held her close.

"Lady, it's okay. He was shot too," she said and squirmed out of my grasp to point at Haynes, lying motionless about fifteen feet away. "You gonna be okay?"

"Probably. Don't worry about me, how are you?"

"Alive. Free."

I smiled and stroked her hair. "Cordell will be so happy to see you." Shock set in even though my wound wasn't that severe and blood loss was minimal, but the pain was a solid nine.

"You know my brother?"

"Just a little," I winced when I tried to sit up and she helped me. "I know he's been looking for you for a long time."

The sound of dozens of motorcycles drowned out my words and I fell backwards, letting my eyes fall closed because I was too tired, too weak to do more. "You should find him."

The last thing I heard was Cross calling out my name.

CREATIVELY CRUSHED

***

"Moon, wake up!" Despite his gruff voice, Cross's hands were gentle as they brushed my hair from my face. "Moon, please open your eyes." His voice was more tortured than I'd ever heard it. I struggled to open my eyes, not even sure where I was only that my back was no longer pressed against the hard concrete outside the clubhouse.

"Cross." My words came easily though my mouth was a little dry. "Beau. Where's Beau?"

"He's fine. Cuddled up with Jana and worried as hell about you."

I hated the thought of Beau worrying over losing his only parent, but I felt fine. A little stiff and my side hurt like crazy but I was fine.

"Ah!" Okay so sitting up hurt a little more than I realized and I fell back against something soft but not quite soft enough. My eyes opened and the first thing I saw was a handsome worried face looking down at me with tired eyes the color of sapphires, relief shining brightly.

"I'm okay, Cross."

He shook his head; chocolate hair tousled, no doubt from raking his hand through it too many times, brushed against his collar as he leaned forward to press his forehead against mine.

"Fuck, Moon. I thought I lost you."

"Cross." The emotion in my voice reflected what was written all over his face. Affection, maybe more. Possibly more. Hopefully more. "I'm fine."

"You're not fine, dammit. You have twenty-nine fucking stitches." His big hand caressed my face and I could see the agony twisting his rugged features. "I'm sorry I wasn't there."

I smacked at his hand until he pulled back with a frown. "I'm not, Cross. You were exactly where you needed to be."

"No—"

CREATIVELY CRUSHED

"No! It's time for me to talk. Did you take care of Roadkill? Because as much as it hurt getting shot and as frickin' terrified as I was during those endlessly long minutes with Detective Haynes, it's all worth it if this shit is over. So, did you?"

I nodded. "White Boy Craig and his crew were arrested and most of them are handcuffed to hospital beds somewhere in this fucking place." I could see him struggling with how much to tell me and I smiled.

"Spit it out, Cross."

His grin was sheepish, but he took my hand in his and pressed my palm against his cheek. I let my thumb graze the scruff on his jawline.

"Craig was injured bad, a bullet in each knee. Lu, the guy dating Pacheco's daughter is gone." He rattled off each injury or fatality and I could see the toll it all took on him.

"What about the Reckless Bastards?" Holding my breath, I waited for him to say a name that was familiar to me, which at this point was all of them.

"Max took a bullet in the shoulder, but it went straight through and he's already bitching about the pain meds. Savior got shot dead on, but his vest kept him alive. He'll be bruised, but he's fine. I'm more worried about you."

I frowned at his words. "How long have I been in here?" Which I finally realized was a tiny hospital room with just a single bed.

"About six hours. You hit your head pretty bad when you fell on the concrete. When I found you, Jessica was cradling your head in her lap crying her little heart out. She wouldn't let anyone touch you—or her."

"Jessica! Where is she? Is she all right?" My heart leapt at the image she'd presented, dirty and frail, terrified. "Can I see her?"

Cross smiled and leaned in to give me a kiss that reminded me I was a little banged up but still very much alive. "She's been pacing outside for the past six hours. Won't even talk to the Feds until she can see

CREATIVELY CRUSHED

you." He smirked and helped me sit up in bed. "You must've made quite an impression."

It was more like I was the first friendly face she'd seen in almost a year. "She was so scared, Cross. The things she must have seen." I couldn't even imagine what had been done to her during the months she'd been a victim of Roadkill MC. I watched Cross take a few steps to the door and when he returned there was a parade of people behind him.

"Ms. Moon!" Jessica pushed around Cross and fell against the bed, lying her still dirty blond hair on my lap, sobbing when I began caressing her soft hair. "You saved me!"

"No honey, you saved yourself. Think of all the girls who didn't make it and remember why you did." She was just a kid. Fresh faced with a hint of naivete, I hoped she would be all right. "I'm so happy you're okay, Jessica."

"Call me Jessie."

"And you can call me Moon." I wrapped my arms around her frail body and held on tight while she sobbed and sobbed against me. "You're okay now, sweet girl."

She pulled back so I could see her face and I gasped at all the crusted blood all over her face, her hair and the much too sexy dress she wore. "It was so scary," she whispered.

"Sorry to interrupt but we really need to speak with Jessica." The voice belonged to a tall man with graying brown hair, beside him a petite woman wearing the same government issue suit and stoic expression.

"We need to speak with both of you," another voice sounded but though I recognized the voice, I couldn't see the sneering little face that belonged to it.

"What is he doing here?" Dodds was Haynes' partner and I wanted nothing to do with either of them.

Cross stepped forward and took my hand. "Dodds was the one who took Haynes out."

CREATIVELY CRUSHED

Oh. "What? Why?"

He smiled. "Because that's what Internal Affairs does, ma'am."

I smiled at the irony and relaxed against the cheap hospital mattress with Jessica on one side and Cross on the other, the two flanking me protectively. "You certainly took your role to heart, Detective."

"Yeah, thanks. I'm sorry you got shot Ms. Vanderbilt but I didn't have a clear shot without hitting the girl. I did my best, and then you jumped, and well, the rest is history."

"No apology necessary, Detective. You had a job to do and I'm glad you took it seriously." I felt myself getting drowsy again when it occurred to me that I probably had a concussion. "Wow who would've thought?" I groaned and squeezed Cross's hand.

"Beau?"

"I'll take care of him, sweetheart. Get some rest."

Sweetheart.

"You know, it's too damn bad you're not over your wife yet, 'cause I love you."

CREATIVELY CRUSHED

Chapter Twenty-Nine

Cross

Too damn bad you're not over your wife yet, 'cause I love you. Even a week later Moon's words kept replaying in my mind over and over like a song I couldn't get out of my head. I couldn't decide if that was a good thing or bad.

Moon said she loved me and I knew she didn't make that declaration lightly even if it had come at the oddest fucking time. I knew she wouldn't have said it if she didn't mean it, which meant I needed to figure my shit out. I knew how I felt about Moon—I loved her too—but I also didn't know if I was the best thing for her. Or Beau.

Especially after I told her what I came to say.

"Cross, why are you standing out here by yourself?" Beau opened the door and looked up at me with a quizzical expression on his face.

"I guess I was lost in thought. Can I come in?" Instead of answering, the kid grabbed my hand and pulled me inside.

"Mom will be happy to see you, she's been kind of sad. And my grandpa is here. He's so cool. I've never met him before, but he's here now. You want to meet him?" Beau kept up both sides of the conversation as he pulled me through the house almost too fast to notice the large comfortable-looking sectional that now occupied most of the living room. "Where have you been?"

I laughed at his questions. The kid was so much like his mom it wasn't even funny. "Well, I had to deal with some things before I came by to see you guys. Did you miss me?"

Beau nodded but his recently cut hair no longer fell into his inquisitive blue eyes. "I did. I think Mom did, too."

I hoped she did, but when I stepped out back and saw a man sitting beside her, I knew all hope was lost.

CREATIVELY CRUSHED

"Mom look who's here! Grandpa look!"

Both heads turned to face me and I froze at the older man beside her with the same green eyes as Moon.

"Is everything okay?" This guy was a major player on the world stage and he sat beside Moon like it was the most normal thing in the world.

She smiled and tried to stand but I was at her side in two large leaps.

"Thanks, Cross. I'm fine, just a little sore. Still." She turned to the man with a wary smile. "Cross this is my father, Les Collinswood. Daddy this is Cross."

Damn, Les Collinswood was her father? "Nice to meet you."

He eyed me like I might slide that Rolex off his wrist but his slow perusal turned into a smile.

"Captain Wylie, nice to meet you, too. Thank you for keeping my daughter and grandson safe through this unfortunate event."

He was thanking me when I was the reason they were in danger in the first place? Maybe Moon wasn't the one who hit her head after all, maybe it was me?

"Of course. I wouldn't let anything happen to them."

He shook his head. "Your men did a damn fine job of bringing down Pacheco, son. It's too bad about those explosives, though." My heart sank at his words. If he knew, then Moon already knew, too.

"Yeah, that's what I came to talk to you about, Moon."

"About what?" She looked from her father to me with confusion in her eyes. "Someone better tell me something before I get upset."

I looked at her father for a brief second before turning to Moon. "I came here to talk to you and Beau. To see you guys one last time before they take me to jail."

"What? Jail, no!" Her hands reached out to me, grabbing handfuls of my shirt and pulling me close. "No, why?"

My heart ached at her pain, caused again by me. "Because our diversionary tactics were unappreciated by law enforcement and when you factor in that Haynes met his demise on club property, well I'm up a creek without a big enough paddle."

"So you're really going to jail?"

I nodded. "Tanya has been working her ass off but nothing has worked, that's why I haven't been by in a few days. I knew it would hurt too much but I had to come today to tell you that you were right. I do still love my wife and I always will, but I'm ready to move on, and I'm crazy in love with you."

She sniffled and looked up. "You are?"

A loud laugh burst out of me. "Yeah, I am. I've been too busy feeling sorry for myself and checking out of everything but the club until you came along with your deep breathing and yoga. Pilates and chickpea burgers and that fuckin'—oops sorry, sir—blueberry wine. I love every weird thing about you, every quirk and every one of those damn jangling bracelets." I kissed one cheek and then the other. "And your never ending supply of colorful dresses, everything about you sucked me in and made me want to live again."

"I did all that?"

"You did. You and Beau. And I screwed it up. Put you guys in danger and then I wasn't there for you when you needed me."

She growled and shook her head. "It's not your responsibility to save the whole world, Cross. Why am I doomed to love men with a huge savior complex?"

"You still love me?"

"Of course I do, you big lug. And you're leaving me." Tears pooled in her eyes and I felt terrible. But when she held strong, refusing to let the tears fall, she ripped my heart right out of my chest.

"Tanya is hopeful that we can make a deal, especially considering the whole dirty cops and politicians thing." I didn't tell her that a good deal still meant a few years behind bars.

Moon's father cleared his throat to get our attention. "Actually, that's the other reason I'm here."

"It is?" Moon seemed as surprised as I was.

Les nodded, smiling down at Beau who'd grabbed his hand and held it tight. I knew that feeling well, the old man was a goner already. "I'm so proud of you honey, you handled Hanes beautifully."

"Daddy," she cried and went to him, hugging him tight. "I've always wanted to hear you say you're proud of me."

"I am proud of you, honey. It was the right thing to do and also why I'm here today." It was clear we were both confused but Les was a man who moved in his own time and we just had to wait. "Anytime explosives are involved, we worry about national security. But when I arrived in town and got the lay of the land, I knew I had to intervene."

"Daddy, *you're* putting him in prison?"

Hurt flashed in his eyes but his smile was bittersweet, making me wonder what had torn this father-daughter relationship apart. "No, Carolina—I mean Moon—I'm not. I did however stop by to see the prosecutor in this case before I came over here, and I made her see the dangers of prosecuting the man who uncovered this scandal and saved hundreds of victims of human trafficking."

Shit. "You didn't have to do that."

"Damn right I did. What you did was commendable and should not be punished and if I have a say in this—which I do—it won't be." He shook his head in disgust. "A politician involved in trafficking? I'll make sure Pacheco gets locked up tight, don't worry about that."

Moon's dad was a straight up gangster in a three-piece suit. I knew he'd make good on his promise. "I don't know how to thank you for this, Mr. Collinswood." I held my hand out, shocked as shit that he hadn't thrown my dirty biker ass out of the house, but he took it and gave a strong shake just as I expected from a man of his significance.

"None necessary, just take care of my baby girl and her son. I'll handle Pacheco and if you need any help, don't be afraid to reach out."

"Not a problem, sir."

"Not at all," Moon said as she stepped into my arms. "We take care of each other around here, though. None of that macho crap."

"Hey! We're men, Mom. We are macho!" Beau flexed his muscles in a way that I knew was purely Max's influence but drew a laugh from each of us all the same. "Right, Grandpa?"

Even the old man wasn't immune to Beau's charms, smiling wide with a distinct glassiness in his eyes.

With Moon in my arms and Beau looking up at me like I hung the moon, the sun and the stars, it was a damn good feeling. One I never thought I'd ever feel again. The love of a damn fine woman and the most adorable little boy on the planet. One who'd finally kicked his asthma to the curb.

What in the fuck did I do to get so lucky?

I guess even the rottenest of Bastards get a second chance at love.

* * * *

~ THE END ~

Acknowledgements

Thank you so much for making my books a success! I appreciate all of you! Thanks to all of my beta readers, street teamers, ARC readers and Facebook fans. Y'all are THE BEST!

And a huge very special thanks to Jessie! I'm such a *hot mess, but without your keen sense of organization and skills, I'd be a burny fiery inferno of hot mess!! Thank you!

And a very special thanks to my editors (who sometimes have to work all through the night! *See HOT MESS above!) Thank you for making my words make sense.

Copyright © 2018 KB Winters and BookBoyfriends Publishing LLC

KB WINTERS

About The Author

KB Winters is a Wall Street Journal and USA Today Bestselling Author of steamy hot books about Bikers, Billionaires, Bad Boys and Badass Military Men. Just the way you like them. She has an addiction to caffeine, tattoos and hard-bodied alpha males. The men in her books are very sexy, protective and sometimes bossy, her ladies are…well…*bossier*!

Living in sunny Southern California, with her five kids and three fur babies, this embarrassingly hopeless romantic writes every chance she gets!

You can reach me at Facebook.com/kbwintersauthor and at kbwintersauthor@gmail.com

Copyright © 2018 KB Winters and BookBoyfriends Publishing LLC

Printed in Great Britain
by Amazon